BOOK**SHOTS**

AVAILABLE NOW!

CROSS KILL

Along Came a Spider killer Gary Soneji died years ago. But Alex Cross swears he sees Soneji gun down his partner. Is his greatest enemy back from the grave?

ZOO 2

Humans are evolving into a savage new species that could save civilization—or end it. James Patterson's *Zoo* was just the beginning.

THE TRIAL

An accused killer will do anything to disrupt his own trial, including a courtroom shocker that Lindsay Boxer and the Women's Murder Club will never see coming.

LITTLE BLACK DRESS

Can a little black dress change everything? What begins as one woman's fantasy is about to go too far.

THE WITNESSES

The Sanderson family has been forced into hiding after one of them stumbled upon a criminal plot. Or so they think. No one will answer their questions. And the terrifying truth may come too late....

LET'S PLAY MAKE-BELIEVE

Christy and Marty just met, and it's love at first sight. Or is it? One of them is playing a dangerous game—and only one will survive.

CHASE

A man falls to his death in an apparent accident.... But why does he have the fingerprints of another man who is already dead? Detective Michael Bennett is on the case.

HUNTED

Someone is luring men from the streets to play a mysterious, high-stakes game. Former Special Forces officer David Shelley goes undercover to shut it down—but will he win?

113 MINUTES

Molly Rourke's son has been murdered. Now she'll do whatever it takes to get justice. No one should underestimate a mother's love....

$10,000,000 MARRIAGE PROPOSAL

A mysterious billboard offering $10 million to get married intrigues three single women in LA. But who is Mr. Right...and is he the perfect match for the lucky winner?

FRENCH KISS

It's hard enough to move to a new city, but now everyone French detective Luc Moncrief cares about is being killed off. Welcome to New York.

TAKING THE TITANIC

Posing as newlyweds, two ruthless thieves board the Titanic to rob its well-heeled passengers. But an even more shocking plan is afoot...

KILLER CHEF

Caleb Rooney knows how to do two things: run a food truck and solve a murder. When people suddenly start dying of food-borne illnesses, the stakes are higher than ever....

THE CHRISTMAS MYSTERY

Two stolen paintings disappear from a Park Avenue murder scene—French detective Luc Moncrief is in for a merry Christmas.

BLACK & BLUE

Detective Harry Blue is determined to take down the serial killer who's abducted several women, but her mission leads to a shocking revelation.

COME AND GET US

When an SUV deliberately runs Miranda Cooper and her husband off a desolate Arizona road, she must run for help alone as his cryptic parting words echo in her head: "Be careful who you trust."

PRIVATE: THE ROYALS

After kidnappers threaten to execute a Royal Family member in front of the Queen, Jack Morgan and his elite team of PIs have just twenty-four hours to stop them. Or heads will roll…literally.

LEARNING TO RIDE

City girl Madeline Harper never wanted to love a cowboy. But rodeo king Tanner Callen might change her mind…and win her heart.

THE McCULLAGH INN IN MAINE

Chelsea O'Kane escapes to Maine to build a new life—until she runs into Jeremy Holland, an old flame.…

SACKING THE QUARTERBACK

Attorney Melissa St. James wins every case. Now, when she's up against football superstar Grayson Knight, her heart is on the line, too.

THE MATING SEASON

Documentary ornithologist Sophie Castle is convinced that her heart belongs only to the birds—until she meets her gorgeous cameraman, Rigg Greensman.

THE RETURN

Ashley Montoya was in love with Mack McLeroy in high school—until he broke her heart. But when an accident brings him back home to Sunnybell to recover, Ashley can't help but fall into his embrace....

BODYGUARD

Special Agent Abbie Whitmore has only one task: protect Congressman Jonathan Lassiter from a violent cartel's threats. Yet she's never had to do it while falling in love....

DAZZLING: THE DIAMOND TRILOGY, BOOK I

To support her artistic career, Siobhan Dempsey works at the elite Stone Room in New York...never expecting to be swept away by Derick Miller.

RADIANT: THE DIAMOND TRILOGY, BOOK II

After an explosive breakup with her billionaire boyfriend, Siobhan moves to Detroit to pursue her art. But Derick isn't ready to give her up.

HOT WINTER NIGHTS

Allie Thatcher moved to Montana to start fresh as the head of the Bear Mountain trauma center. And even though the days are cold, the nights are steamy...especially when she meets search-and-rescue leader Dex Belmont.

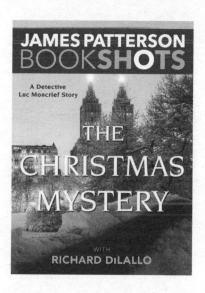

BLACK & BLUE

JAMES PATTERSON
WITH CANDICE FOX

BOOKSHOTS

Little, Brown and Company

New York Boston London

Copyright © 2016 by James Patterson

BookShots / Little, Brown and Company
Hachette Book Group
1290 Avenue of the Americas, New York, NY 10104
bookshots.com

First North American Edition: December 2016
Originally published in Great Britain by Random House UK, June 2016.

BookShots is an imprint of Little, Brown and Company, a division of Hachette Book Group, Inc. The Little, Brown name and logo are trademarks of Hachette Book Group, Inc. The BookShots name and logo are trademarks of JBP Business, LLC.

The Hachette Speakers Bureau provides a wide range of authors for speaking events. To find out more, go to hachettespeakersbureau.com or call (866) 376-6591.

ISBN 978-0-316-39918-0 / 978-0-316-50626-7 (Walmart edition)
LCCN 2016938290

10 9 8 7 6 5 4 3 2 1

LSC-C

Printed in the United States of America

BLACK & BLUE

CHAPTER 1

I'M AN EXPERIENCED hunter of humans. It's not hard, if you understand how they think. People have tunnel vision and are objective-driven. As long as you don't interfere with their goal, and don't make yourself known before you're ready to pounce, you can close in on a relaxed target pretty easily. It doesn't even require much stealth. Unlike animals, human beings don't use their alarm system of senses. Though the wind was behind me, Ben Hammond didn't smell me. He didn't hear my breath over the clunk of his boots on the pavement.

Hammond's objective was his late-model Honda Civic on the edge of the parking lot. So that's all he could see—he didn't notice me round the corner from the loading dock and fall into step behind him. He left the shopping center with hands full of groceries swinging at his sides and headed across the parking lot, already sliding into the driver's seat in his mind, shutting the door on the moonless night.

I followed with my head down, my hoodie pulled up against the security cameras trained on the few remaining cars. I let him pull his keys out of his pocket, the jangling sound covering the soft fall of my boots for the last few steps between me and my prey.

I closed the distance and attacked.

CHAPTER 2

"FUCK!" BEN HAMMOND grabbed at the back of his head where I'd punched him, turned and stumbled against the car, dropping the bags. Glass cracked in one of them. He cowered in a half-crouch, trying to make himself smaller. Both hands shot up. "Oh, my God! What are you doing?"

"Stand up." I waved impatiently.

"Take—m-my—wallet," he stammered. "Don't hurt m—"

"You don't like the surprise attack, do you, Ben? You know how effective it is."

He realized three things very quickly. First, that I was a woman. Second, that this wasn't a mugging. Third, that he'd heard my voice before.

The man straightened almost fully and squinted into the darkness of my hood. I tugged the hood down and watched his eyes wander around the silhouette of my short hair against the shopping-center lights, the terror in his face slowly dissipating.

"I…" He straightened. His hands dropped. "I know you."

"You do."

"You're that cop." He pointed an uncertain finger at me, began to shake it as his confidence grew. "You're that cop from the trial."

"I am," I said. "Detective Harriet Blue, here to deliver your punishment."

CHAPTER 3

IT WAS A little insulting that my name didn't come to Ben's mind as quickly as I'd hoped. But I had just cracked him on the skull. What little gray matter was sloshing around his brain probably needed time to recover. I'd done everything I could to make him aware of me while he was tried for the rape of his ex-girlfriend Molly. When I took the stand to testify that I'd found Molly at the bottom of the shower where he'd dumped her, I'd looked right at him and calmly and clearly stated my name.

It hadn't been a solid case. Ben had been very crafty in getting back at his ex for leaving him: raping and beating her, but charming his way into her apartment struggle-free and sharing a glass of wine with her first, so it looked as if she'd welcomed the sexual encounter. I'd known, sitting on the witness stand and staring at him, that like most rapists he'd probably go free.

But that didn't mean I was finished with him.

"This is assault." Ben touched the back of his head, noted the blood on his fingers, and almost smiled. "You're in a lot of trouble, you stupid little bitch."

"Actually," I slid my right foot back, "*you're* in a lot of trouble."

I gave Ben a couple of sharp jabs to the face, then backed up, let him have a moment to feel them. He stepped out from between the shopping bags and came at me swinging. I sidestepped and planted my knee in his ribs, sending him sprawling on the asphalt. I glanced at the distant shopping center. The security guards would notice a commotion at the edge of the farthest parking lot camera and come running. I figured I had seconds, not minutes.

"You can't do this." Hammond spat blood from his split lip. "You—"

I gave him a knee to the ribs, then lifted him before he could get a lungful of air and slammed him into the car's hood. I'm petite, but I box, so I know how to maneuver a big opponent. I grabbed a handful of Ben's hair and dragged him towards the driver's door.

"You're a cop!" Hammond wailed.

"You're right," I said. I could just make out two security guards rushing out of the loading dock.

"My job gives me access to crime alerts," I said. "I can tag a person's file and get a notification every time they're brought in, even if their original charge never stuck."

I held on to Hammond's hair and gave him a couple of hard punches in the head, then dumped him onto the ground. The guards were closer. I stepped on Hammond's balls, so I knew I had his full attention.

"If I ever see your name in the system again," I told him, "I'm coming back. And I won't be this gentle next time."

I pulled my hood up and sprinted into the bushes at the side of the lot.

CHAPTER 4

I'M NOT A vigilante. Sometimes I just have no choice but to take matters into my own hands.

I'd worked in sex crimes for five years, and I was tired of seeing predators walking free from convictions. When I got close to a victim, the way I did with Molly Finch, I found it hard to sleep after their attacker was acquitted. For weeks I'd lain awake at night thinking about Hammond's smug face as he'd walked down the steps of the courthouse on Goulburn Street, the wink he'd given me as he got into the taxi. I'd managed to make a minor physical assault charge stick. But there had been no proving *beyond a reasonable doubt* that the sex Hammond had had with Molly that night hadn't been consensual.

That's how it goes sometimes with sexual assaults. The guy's lawyer throws everything he has at the idea that she might have wanted it. There was no physical evidence, or witnesses, to say otherwise.

Well, now there was no evidence to say Ben Hammond wasn't bashed half to death by a mugger gone nuts, either. If he went to the cops about what I'd done, he'd know what it felt like not to be believed.

But he wouldn't go to the cops and tell them a woman had given him a beatdown. His kind never did.

I rolled my shoulders as I drove back across the city towards Potts Point, sighing long and low as the tension eased. I was really looking forward to getting some sleep. Most nights saw me at my local gym pounding boxing bags to try to exhaust myself into a healthy presleep calm. Smacking Ben around had given me the same delicious fatigue in my muscles. I hoped it lasted.

At the big intersection near Kings Cross, a pair of hookers strutted across the road in front of my car. Their skin was lit pink by the huge neon Coca-Cola sign on the corner. The streets were still damp from a big storm the night before. The gutters were crowded with trash and huge fig-tree leaves.

My phone rang. I recognized the number as my station chief.

"Hello, Pops," I said.

"Blue, take down this address," the old man said. "There's a body I want you to look at."

CHAPTER 5

MURDER WAS HARD work, but Hope had never been afraid of that.

She knelt on the floor of the kitchen of the *Dream Catcher* and scrubbed at the polished boards. She was trying to push her brush down the cracks and bring up the blood that had dried and settled there. *Deck,* she thought suddenly, dunking the brush in the bucket of hot water and bleach beside her. On yachts, the floor was not a floor at all but a deck. The kitchen was called a *galley*. She smiled. She'd need to get used to all the terminology. There was so much to learn, being a new boat owner. She sat back on her heels and wiped the sweat from her brow. She'd give the blood a rest for a while and work on the bedroom.

The young woman climbed backwards down the little ladder and walked into the yacht's expansive bedroom, gathering up a garbage bag from the roll she'd placed on the bed. The first thing she did was take a framed photograph from the nightstand and dump it in the darkness of the bag. She didn't look at the couple's smiling faces. She threw in some reading glasses, a pair of slippers, and a folded newspaper. She opened the cupboard and started taking out the woman's clothes, grabbing great handfuls on coat hangers and bundling the shirts, skirts, and pants into a roll before she shoved them into the bag.

Jenny Spelling had awful taste, Hope thought, glancing at a turquoise skirt-suit before it went into the trash. Ugh, shoulder pads. So eighties. She felt a wave of excitement roll over her as she looked along the empty hanging rod, thinking about her own clothes racked there.

When she'd filled all the garbage bags on the rolls with their possessions, Hope walked to the back of the boat to check on her prisoners. The couple was slumped in the corner of the shower cubicle, Jenny's head twisted back against the wall so that her nose pointed upward and her mouth hung open. When Hope opened the door, Ken shifted up as much as his binds would allow. His wife was limp against him.

"I'm just heading out to get rid of some garbage," Hope said brightly. "You guys need anything before I go? More water?"

Jenny Spelling woke and immediately started shivering. She stared at Hope wordlessly, as though she didn't know what the young woman was.

"Hope." Ken's face reddened with desperation. "I'm begging you, please, just take the boat. Take everything. My wife needs to do her dialysis or she's going to die. Okay? It's only going to take a few minutes. That's all. That—"

"We've discussed this." Hope held up her hand, gave him a weary sigh. "It'll all be over soon. I'm not getting into this again. The last time I let you loose, you did this." She held up her forearm, showed him the bruise. "*Trust,* Ken. You had it, and you lost it."

"Please, please." Ken shifted. "You don't need to do this. Look at her. Look at her face. She's missed her dialysis for three days now. She's not right. She's—"

Hope took the duct tape from the counter beside the toilet and ripped off a length. She placed a strip over Jenny's mouth, but gave Ken a few turns around his head. He was the feisty one. She worked emotionlessly as the tape sealed off his words.

"She's gonna die!" the man howled through the tape. "Please!"

CHAPTER 6

HEADING TO THE crime scene, I drove through the quiet streets of Picnic Point and up through the national park. The dark hills were spotted here and there with the gold porch lights of suburban mansions. I'd spent some time out here as a preteen with one of the foster families who had taken on my brother Sam and me. That is, before their adoption dream had ended.

There had been so many young families who'd attempted to integrate us that it was difficult to decide which one it had been. All I remembered was the local school and the crowds of teens in green and gold uniforms, the curious glances we'd received as we entered midway through the semester.

As usual, Sam and I had only been at the school for a few weeks. As a pair of kids who'd been in the system since we were practically toddlers, we didn't make life easy for our foster parents with our bad behavior. It was probably me who had broken the spell by running away in the middle of the night. Or maybe it was Sam setting something on fire, or running his mouth at our potential new parents. We'd both been equally bad at school—fighting off kids who wanted to give us grief, trying to show our new teachers who was really boss. Once our new mommies and daddies realized we weren't grateful for being "saved," the fantasy usually died. In truth, Sam and I had always preferred the group homes and institutions they shipped us to between potential adopters. More places to hide. I dreamed as I drove by the lamplit houses of what it might have been like to grow up here, if I'd been a more stable kid.

The police tape started at the edge of the main road. I was stopped by a young officer in a raincoat and flashed him my badge, only then realizing that my knuckles were still wrapped.

"Okay, Detective Blue, head down to the end of this road where it turns to dirt and go left along the river. You'll see the lights," the cop said.

"The river? Shit!" I felt the fine hairs on my arms stand on end. "Who's the victim?"

The cop waved me on. Another car was coming up behind me. I stood on the gas and zipped down the slope, almost swerving on the corner where the dirt began. I couldn't wait to get to the crime scene. If the victim was a young woman, it meant the Georges River Killer had struck again.

And I was going to get him this time.

CHAPTER 7

I PARKED CLOSE, unwrapped my knuckles, and strode up to the crime scene with my heart pumping in my ears. I didn't even bring my scene kit. I had to know as much as I could, as fast as possible, so that I could get Pops to put me on the case. The Georges River killings were splashed all over the newspapers, and so were the idiots who had control of the case—a group of loutish guys from Sydney Metro Homicide who wouldn't give me so much as a whiff of what they had.

I didn't want the notoriety these cops seemed to enjoy so much. I wanted to be involved in catching what was probably the most savage serial killer in our nation's history. Young, beautiful university students were going missing from the hip urban suburbs around the University of Sydney campus. Their savaged bodies were turning up on the banks of the Georges River three or four days after they disappeared. My brother spent two days of his working week teaching undergrad design students at the university, and lived in their midst in the hip suburbs around Newtown and Broadway. I'd talked to Sam about it a lot, about how the girls in his apartment building were terrified, begging the landlord to put cameras up outside the block, walking each other to and from their cars in the late hours.

It might have been arrogant, or naive, but I felt as if there was something I could contribute. Though my conviction rate in sex crimes wasn't good, that was part of the culture of the court system. I was a good cop, and I could practically smell the Georges River Killer haunting the women of my city. When the police came knocking on that evil prick's door, I wanted to be right there to see his face.

The first thing I noticed that was wrong with the scene was the edge of the police tape. It was far too crowded. Half the officers who should have been in the inner cordon were standing at the outer cordon, talking and smoking in the dark. I recognized a photographer from my station loitering uselessly by the lights rigged up over the scene. A fingerprints specialist was sitting under a tree eating a burrito out of a paper roll. What the hell was everyone doing? I ducked under the tape and came up beside the only officer in the crime scene. He was crouched over the body.

When he turned around, I saw that the man by the body was Tate Barnes.

The walking embodiment of career suicide.

CHAPTER 8

THE EFFECT OF seeing Tate Barnes right in the middle of what I already considered my crime scene was like being maced. My eyes stung and my throat closed with panic. I'd never met the man before, but I knew the shaggy blond hair and the leather jacket from stories I'd heard. There were hundreds of variations on the story of Tate Barnes. It was a terrible tale about a crime the man had committed that he'd tried to hide from the bosses during his academy application. It was said that, as a child, Tate and a group of his friends had murdered a mother and her young son.

I turned away and grabbed at my face, tried to suppress a groan. I needed this guy out of my crime scene. Now. He straightened and offered me his hand.

"I'm Tox Barnes," he rasped. It sounded as though his throat was lined with sandpaper.

"You actually introduce yourself as 'Tox'?"

"I find it minimizes confusion."

I'd heard the nickname, but I hadn't expected him to embrace it. Officers called Barnes "Toxic" because any officer who agreed to work with him was essentially committing themselves to a lifetime of punishment from their fellow officers. General consensus was that Tox

Barnes should never have been allowed into the force. Those who had worked with him were harassed relentlessly by their peers. He was the fox in the henhouse. Aligning yourself with him meant you were on the side of a predator.

I'd heard that there was nothing the administration had been able to do to stop Barnes from being a cop. He'd aced his application, and he'd committed the murders so young his record had been expunged. But that didn't mean the rest of the force was going to sit by and let a murderer operate in their midst. He was the enemy, and if you joined him, you were the enemy, too.

"Listen, Tox, I'm Detective Harriet Blue." I shook his rough hand half-heartedly. "I'm going to need you to clear out of this scene. Chief Morris has put me on it."

"Meh," Tox said, and returned to crouching.

I waited, but nothing further came, so I bent down beside him and glanced at the body.

"Sorry, I didn't catch that."

"I said, 'Meh,'" Tox replied. "It was a dismissive noise."

I was so shocked, so furious, I hadn't even taken in the sight of the girl on the sand before us. My eyes flicked over her naked chest, unseeing, as I tried to get my mind around the reality of the situation. She looked midtwenties, beautiful, dark-haired. She was wearing only a pair of panties. She was a Georges River girl. I knew it. I needed to get this parasite of a man off my case.

"You don't understand," I said, "this is my crime scene. This is my case. And I don't work with partners."

"Neither do I," he said, as if it were a matter of choice.

"Right." I sighed. "So you can give me a brief on what you've observed, and then I need you to beat it and take your dismissive noises with you."

Tox seemed to smirk in the dark as he stood and walked around the back of the body. I couldn't tell if he'd heard me or not. At the edge of the police tape, twenty yards away, my fellow officers were watching carefully to see if I'd cooperate with their nemesis, thereby giving them permission to make my life a living hell. I noticed some journalists among the crowd. The uniformed patrol officers securing the scene were so interested in Tox and me that they weren't even pushing them back.

When I turned around, I saw that Tox had a pocket knife. He flicked open the blade with a snap, and slashed at the girl.

CHAPTER 9

"WHAT THE–" I stood up, tried to shield what Tox was doing from the press, who'd started snapping pictures. "What the fuck are you doing?"

Tox didn't answer. He flipped the girl onto her front and pulled the underpants he'd slashed from her hips off her body. I watched in horror as he poked at the corpse's backside with the butt of the blade. He leaned in close and examined the surface of her skin. Someone at the edge of the crowd sneered.

"Sicko," somebody said. "Someone say something."

"Nah, man. Leave him. Let him mess up all the evidence."

"Detective Barnes," I said, "I'm ordering you to stop what you're doing *right now*."

Tox put both his hands on the corpse's back and pushed down hard, just once. He pulled the hair away from the girl's face and stuck his third finger between her lips, pushed it deep inside her throat. The dead girl's cheeks puckered obscenely to allow his finger to push down. He extracted the finger and looked at the tip in the torchlight, grunted thoughtfully. I watched him take the girl's wrist and give it an exploratory wiggle before he stood up and dusted off his palms.

"Mmm," he said, and strode away from me towards the riverbank.

I followed, grateful to be out of earshot of the vile things the cops at the tape were saying about him. I caught him at the water's edge and shoved him hard in the back. He stumbled in the sand.

"What was that for?" he said in his strange, whispery voice.

"Jesus, I don't know, for violating the corpse of a young woman in front of all the nation's leading newspapers and half the police force?" I snarled. "What is wrong with you, man?"

"I wasn't violating the corpse, I was testing a theory." He looked towards the mouth of the river. "The kids who found the body said they thought they recognized the girl from a party last night, a few streets back from the river. I wanted to find out if that was bullshit before we go off interviewing all the morons who attended the party. She wasn't there. So we can forget that."

I felt as if I were dreaming. This man seemed to have no idea how inappropriate his handling of the body had been. He was looking off towards the river and talking to himself as though I wasn't standing there.

"Of course she wasn't at the party," I said. "Are you *that* stupid? She's a Georges River girl. Right river, right age, right placement of the body. I could have told you that before you stuck your finger in her mouth."

"Are *you* that stupid?" Tox looked at me finally. "She's *not* one of the Georges River Killer's victims. No. She didn't die anywhere near here."

"You're insane." I waved him away and turned back to the crime scene. "You don't touch a body until forensics is done with it. That's the first thing they teach you on the first day of forensics. You just…you've compromised the case."

I could hardly speak I was so mad. His passive stare made it worse.

"Forensics won't find anything," he said. "She's been in the water for hours."

"I'm not listening to you. I like my job too much."

"Heh," he said. "If you liked your job so much, you wouldn't insist on doing it wrong."

"Fuck you."

"She wasn't killed here. She was killed out at sea. She came here in the storm."

I stopped walking and stared at him.

He stuffed his hands into the pockets of his jacket and looked back with the ease and calm of a madman.

"Bullshit."

"Nope," he said. "She's got mottled livor mortis on her ass and pulmonary edema in her lungs."

He waited, but I wasn't going to give him the satisfaction of asking him to explain how he'd come up with that. He walked towards me and stood over me, as most men do.

"Livor mortis," he said. "The settling and pooling of blood in the veins after de—"

"I know what livor mortis is, asshole."

"Well, you'll know that if a corpse is being tossed around in rough water, the blood doesn't settle, so it never collects," he said. "Except in the ass. Fine skin. Lots of big juicy fat cells. I'd say she's been in the water at least twenty hours. With the storm blowing a westerly, she was likely dumped out there, in the ocean."

"The rigor mortis? Not set?"

"No."

"And the pulmonary edema," I said, feeling my hackles rise again. "The foam in her lu—"

"I know what pulmonary edema is, asshole," Tox said.

"She was alive when she went in," I whispered.

CHAPTER 10

I FOLLOWED TOX back to the body of the girl and stood facing away from the crowd. My mind was swirling. Sure, Tox knew his stuff. He'd already started developing a theory, helping my case enormously within only minutes of the scene being cordoned off. But as I glanced at the cops behind me, I knew I couldn't keep him around much longer or I'd never get the thing solved. Working with Tox Barnes wouldn't throw a wrench into the works. It'd throw a whole toolbox.

As far as I'd heard, people now and then were forced to work with him. But he was a burden that one took heavily, and offloaded as soon as possible. You found a way to transfer out of partnership with him, or soon enough you would begin to find your job almost impossible. People started avoiding you in the coffee room. Losing your reports, delaying your lab results. Accidents would begin to happen—someone would spill coffee on your laptop, bump your car on the way out of the parking lot, forget to include you in weekend get-togethers.

I'd just turned to him to ask him again to leave when I noticed he was smoking a cigarette.

"Jesus Christ," I said. "Put that out! You're in my crime scene."

He grunted.

"You've just had that hand in a dead girl!"

"That was this hand." He lifted the other from his pocket, waved it, pulled the cigarette from his mouth with the clean one. "For a detective, you're pretty blind to details. Me? I've noticed everything there is to notice about your hands. Chewed nails. Swollen knuckles. No sign of a wedding ring, probably ever."

"Look." I leaned close. "I don't like you. I don't want to work with you. I've heard bad things, and they appear to be true. You should have waited for an autopsy to confirm your findings. There's a process, and it's in place for a reason."

"I don't like to waste time," he said. "And that's exactly what you're doing now, jibber-jabbering at me. What station you work at?"

"Surry Hills," I said.

"Right." He clapped me hard on the shoulder as he turned to leave. "I'll see you there first thing."

He wandered off, and the police officers lining the tape watched him go. When he was a good distance away they ducked under the tape and started setting up to do their jobs. I stood stunned in their midst, no idea what I should do next. The photographer snapped a picture of me standing over the body, my arms folded.

"That guy's a murderer, you know," he said, adjusting his lens. "Killed a mother and her young kid. Beat 'em to death. Tox was seven."

"Yeah, so I hear." I was badly craving a cigarette of my own now. I hadn't smoked in years. But no one around me was offering anything but hateful glances.

"Guy like that's gonna do it again," the photographer said. "You don't start that young unless it's in your bones."

CHAPTER 11

MY HEAD WAS a mess by the time I arrived at Surry Hills police headquarters. It was 6 a.m. and the sun was rising. I'd stayed at the crime scene and orchestrated the evidence collection, got rid of the press and sent out a couple of detectives to bring the parents in. Within an hour we had preliminary identification. Until we could get the parents to ID the body, we weren't sure. But it looked as though the girl was Claudia Burrows; her description linked up with a missing persons report that had been issued a day earlier. She had a tattoo of a rabbit in a waistcoat on her hip that matched the report exactly.

I didn't like where this was all going, mainly because it was heading in the very opposite direction to the Georges River Killer. The killer we'd been hunting didn't drown his victims—he didn't put them in the water at all, but left them stripped to their panties, face down on the beach. His victims showed signs of physical and sexual abuse, while Claudia hadn't looked in any way battered. I'd checked her wrists and ankles for ligature marks but there were none, except for a rough sort of rubbing on one foot. For all I knew, she might have fallen into Botany Bay drunk and drowned there, the waves stripping her clothes off as she floated towards the mouth of the river.

Though it didn't look good for my entry onto the Georges River

Killer task force, I wasn't going to let go. It was possible the killer had changed his methods to confuse us. He was a wily creature, as far as I could tell, and he might have recognized that he was being tracked. I went right to the door of the task force's case room and knocked, trying to shove my way in when no one answered. I came up against the thin and wiry Detective Nigel Spader just inside the door.

"You're not allowed in here." He pushed me back out the door before I could get a glimpse of their case board. "This is the last time I'm going to tell you, Blue."

"I'm allowed in," I said. "Chief Morris put me on a Georges River body last night. You'll need to debrief me and get me up to speed so we can start making connections."

"Your case is not connected to ours." He tried to shut the door on me.

"How the fuck would you know something like that? It's a dark-haired girl almost naked on the banks of the Georges. I'm ticking all the boxes. If I knew what other boxes I could tick, maybe the link would be even stronger. You're putting me on this task force, Nigel, before I kick you in the face."

"It's not the GRK." Nigel sighed. "Now piss off."

He slammed the door on my boot. I shoved forward, slid an arm into the gap, and tried to grab him. Pops's voice sent a bolt of electricity through me.

"Detective Blue!"

"I'm just helping, Chief." I pulled the door shut, gave the knob a jiggle. "Making sure the case room is secure."

"You've got the dead girl's parents in interrogation room six." He carried his coffee towards me. "I've put the paperwork in. You'll share the case with Detective Barnes."

"Are you kidding me?"

"He was the first responder," the old man said. "He's got some good theories. The media has got hold of the case already, so it'll be all over the news. And she's a bright, pretty university student. I want to have something meaningful to say at the press conference."

"University student?" My mouth fell open.

"She'd just applied and been accepted. Her parents told the patrol cops who picked them up," the Chief said. "Applied, studied—in the media's eyes, it's the same thing. She was full of prospects. We need to get something quickly."

"Well, you can tell them this is a Georges River Killer case, then." I counted off on my fingers: "Dark hair, Georges River, semi-naked, university student…"

"It's not," Pops said, and walked away.

I stood in the middle of the bullpen and looked at the officers all around me, some of them answering phones, some of them clicking away at computers. Had the whole world gone crazy? I felt as if I were speaking a foreign language, and everyone I talked to was pretending to understand and then brushing me off. I was concerned I was getting so frustrated I might be tempted to cry. I generally cry about once a year, so I wasn't going to waste it on this bureaucratic bullshit.

"This *is* a Georges River Killer case!" I roared. The men and women on their phones turned to look at me. "I need to be on the task force!"

"It's not," Pops said calmly as he closed the door to his office.

CHAPTER 12

THE *DREAM CATCHER* had been in a dry dock at Garden Island for two days. In that time, Hope had cleared it of almost all the Spellings' possessions. She did keep some things—a nice new laptop that had belonged to Ken, and some of Jenny's more modern jewelry. She was exhausted from constant trips to the shower cubicle to see if Ken was awake, and, if he was, to hold the chloroform-soaked rag over his face until he slept again. Jenny didn't stir at all. It was as though she knew her husband was lost in the land of dreams, and she'd chosen to join him there.

Between trips to check on her prisoners, Hope spent most of that morning lying on the bow in one of the deck chairs in her bikini, reading the yacht's operating manual and writing down questions for Ken. She needed a tan if she was going to fit in with the other yachties—she couldn't look like a newbie or they wouldn't accept her into their world. Sometimes she closed her eyes and pretended she was at sea, sailing across the Indian Ocean, the sun baking her pale skin a deep golden brown like Jenny's. She didn't keep her eyes closed too long, or she'd see flashes, electric zings of light that sometimes contained frightened faces, splashes of blood, clawing fingers. The images played about the corners of her eyes, made her chew her nails. They'd go, in time, these memories. She just had to focus on the plan.

It was almost funny, the way it had all come together one night at the Black Garter while she'd been sitting in the window watching the men outside. One of the girls had wandered in from the main hall with a sea captain's hat on her head, tipping the brim in the closet mirror and tilting her naked hips. She'd snagged the hat from the leader of a bachelor party, the pack of drunken boys hollering from the back courtyard as other girls danced around the lazy-eyed groom.

"What do you think?" The girl had taken the cap off and sent it sailing across the room into Hope's hands like a Frisbee. "Captain Hope, reporting for duty."

Hope had stared at herself in the mirror after the girl had gone, the cap too big on her head, a tiny girl playing dress-up. She'd remembered sailing with her father, those few times he had indulged himself over the years and rented cruisers for a trot around the harbor. Pretending he owned them. Lies and make-believe. Hope was so tired of all the games—the ones the men made her play, the ones she played with herself. Captain Hope, Master of Her Own Destiny.

It would take a miracle to achieve something like that, she'd thought. Or would it?

What exactly *would* it take?

Hope walked the length of the vessel now, examining the newly painted surface, and then climbed down the ladder onto the floor of the dry dock. When she'd acquired the *Dream Catcher* it had been a hideous wine-bottle green, but the guys she'd hired for the makeover had finished the last coat of the new color—a chic, modern ash gray.

Hope had started making lists of steps in her plan that very night as she'd huddled away in the back of the brothel, and once the list had been completed, she'd made a new one. She couldn't remember how many lists it had taken, how many crossed or canceled steps. Find a couple selling their yacht. Find an ally to comfort the couple as they inquired about the sale, someone cute and easy to manipulate, someone who knew how to act in a prescribed role. Hope had followed a recipe she found online for chloroform and cooked it in the brothel kitchen, whistling, as if she were baking a cake.

Picking out and commissioning the fresh paint job on the boat was one step she'd been looking forward to for a while. She stood now with her hand on the vessel and listened to the hull to see if there was any sign of the couple from within. Nothing. She wandered around the back of the boat in her sun hat and glasses and stood watching the men on the ladder as they applied the new name to the side.

"Just in time for the big reveal," the tall one said. He was a stunning young man in a cut-off undershirt, spattered all over with tiny spots of white paint. He looked as if he were covered in stars. He reached up and began peeling away the paper stencil around the lettering on the hull of the boat.

"The *New Hope,*" she read. She felt a dark stirring in her chest at the sight of the words. She'd had the boys paint them in a deep crimson. Her dream, written in blood.

CHAPTER 13

TOX WAS ALREADY in the interrogation room with Claudia's parents. Not only was it one of the unfriendliest rooms in the station to speak to them, but I had no idea what he'd already said. I felt my stomach tighten as I spotted him sitting there in the cramped, musty room beyond the two-way mirror, their horrified faces. Mom and Dad had recently been crying. She was a heavy blond woman, and their daughter's lean features and dark hair came from her mustached father. I threw open the door just in time.

"…breast implants?" Tox was saying.

"What?" Mrs. Burrows frowned. She glanced at me, her mouth twisted.

"Yeah, what?" I sat down beside Tox.

"I was just asking Mr. and Mrs. Burrows here how long it had been since their daughter got those breast implants." He looked lazily at me. "You did notice the cadaver had breast implants, right?"

"Mr. and Mrs. Burrows." I put my hands calmly on the table beside the handcuff hooks. "I must apologize for my partner here. Detective Barnes has been under a lot of stress and isn't thinking clearly."

Tox folded his hands on the table beside mine, imitating me. "Look, your daughter was found deceased this morning, and that's very sad. But I'm sure that you'll get over that sadness and want to catch whoever did this, eventually. Well, you know what? *We* want to catch whoever did this *now*. It's our job, see. Now your daughter had fake tits—"

"Tox!" I yelped.

"—and I'm putting together the exaggerated size of those tits, and her petite figure, and the approximate cost of such a surgical enhancement, and your obvious middle-classness—I'm going to take a leap and say she was a prostitute."

"Jesus!" I clapped a hand over my eyes.

"Actually, it's not a leap at all," Tox confirmed. "She *was* a prostitute, wasn't she?"

The Burrowses sat stunned. I got up and grabbed Tox's arm and yanked him towards the door.

"I'll be back," I told the couple. "Just sit tight."

Tox turned on me in the hallway.

"What is it with you and wasting time?" he grunted, almost irritated. "I was on a roll in there."

"You were *not* on a roll," I snapped. "You were on anything but a roll. You were traumatizing the dead girl's parents."

"Jesus Christ!" Tox threw his hands up, flapped them dramatically, trying to imitate my voice with his gravelly tones. "*You're sticking your finger in the dead girl. You're smoking near the dead girl. You're traumatizing the parents of the dead girl.* You sure you're right for this job, Detective? You might find yourself better employed in undertaking. You're in love with the dead girl."

"You just…you can't talk to people this way." I was so horrified, the words wouldn't come. "These parents are grieving. No, they're probably not even grieving yet. They're probably still in shock."

"Is the emotional state of these people really your priority right now?" Tox shook his head in disbelief. "First you want me to slow down so that we can go through all the procedural bullshit surrounding the corpse. Now you want me to slow down so we can go through all the emotional crap with the parents. Do you actually want to solve this case or are you just trying to score overtime?"

"It's not crap, it's…it's life!"

"Not my life," Tox snorted.

A pair of patrol cops were walking down the hall towards us, carrying folders full of papers. One bumped hard into my shoulder as she passed, causing me to drop my phone. My punishment had begun. Nearby, an older officer I knew, Chris Murray, was fielding a call and glaring at us, taking in the figure of my new partner with obvious distaste.

"How long has the couple been missing?" Murray was saying into his mobile. "And what's the name of the boat?"

"Listen," I pointed at Tox, "if we're going to work together on this, there need to be rules. I think number one should be that I do all the talking, all the time."

"Geh," he grunted. "Sounds just like a woman. All the talking, all the time."

He went back into the interrogation room. I held my face in my hands for a long moment, relishing the darkness. When I lifted my head there were about five people in the bullpen staring at me, each set of eyes more hateful than the last.

CHAPTER 14

I CALLED MY brother Sam from the ladies' bathroom, leaning my forehead on the mirror. I knew that he'd probably be teaching his classes at the university, but I dialed anyway.

"What's up?" he answered.

"I'm in crisis mode," I said. "I need a friendly voice."

I explained the situation in a long, rambling stream. In the background of the call I could hear students rumbling through the halls of the university.

"Being partnered up with this guy—is it going to make solving the case difficult?"

"The case should be fine, but my social standing might take a hit."

He laughed. I'd never had many friends to begin with, and he knew that. I was a loner. Hardly a cheerful spirit. I forgot people's birthdays and didn't turn up to work drinks. None of my colleagues tried to set me up on dates. They knew a romantic train wreck when they saw one.

"If I stick with him too long, I might have to start chewing my lunch more carefully," I continued.

"Cops," Sam said. "All that ancient brotherhood bullshit."

"I can see where everyone's coming from." I sighed. "I mean, apart from what he's supposed to have done, the guy is also a world-class arrogant dickhead."

I told Sam about his treatment of Claudia's body, about how he'd spoken to her parents.

"He might just be out of practice on his behavior with other people, if he's such an outcast. He might have genuinely forgotten how people are supposed to talk to each other," Sam suggested.

"You always think the best of people," I said. "I don't know how. I'm about ready to kill him."

"Well, that might make things messier."

"You may be the only man I'm not prepared to strangle right now," I told him. "That detective Nigel Spader caught me at the door to the case room. I didn't even get a peek."

"Ah yes, I've met that one. He was here yesterday doing interviews of the tutors, trying to find out if we know anything about the Georges River girls," Sam said. "I think we're booked in for second interviews today. Two of the victims were students here."

"Second interviews?"

"A couple of us, yeah," he said. "I don't know why."

"Weird. Were the victims students of yours?"

"No." He sighed. "But some of my students were friends with them. A girl rushed out of my morning class yesterday, crying. It's hard to know what to say."

My stomach felt mildly unsettled. I put the phone on speaker and washed my face under the tap.

"Tell me how the second interview goes," I told Sam. I convinced myself it was just the stress of the new case and my new partner making me sick. If I kept on track, it would go away.

As I'd find often in my life, I should have listened to what my instincts were telling me.

CHAPTER 15

TOX SMOKED IN my car. As I drove, I tried to think of one thing about him that didn't annoy me. I decided I didn't mind Tox's leather jacket. I had a similar one. We stopped for coffee outside the station and then headed west towards Claudia Burrows's apartment on Parramatta Road.

"When you arrived at the crime scene last night, I saw you unwrapping your knuckles in your car," Tox said, putting one of his boots on the dashboard. "You box?"

"I box, yes."

"Who'd you beat up?"

"I didn't beat anyone up."

"Boxers spar. There's very little blood involved. Looked to me like you pounded on someone outside the ring, using your boxing skills to get the upper hand."

"See, this is what you do," I said. "You make microscopic observations and you blow them out into wild theories that make no sense."

"Like the tits."

"Stop saying 'tits'! Christ, you sound like a fat, sleazy truck driver in a highway bar." I imitated his quiet, gravelly voice, grabbed my crotch: *"Look at those tits! I love tits! Urgghh!"*

"Was that supposed to be me?"

"Yes."

"You want to know why I sound like this?" he rasped. I glanced over, and he pulled at the collar of his shirt, revealing a long pink scar at the base of his throat. "Drug dealer stabbed me in the neck during a raid. Went right through the windpipe and out the other side."

"Well," I said, "I'm sorry. I didn't mean to make fun."

He stared at me. "What kind of a horrible person makes fun of someone with a physical disabil—"

"Shut up!" I shoved him into the car door. "Goddamnit!"

"All right, so. Mom and Dad claimed Claudia was a part-time waitress," Tox said. "She wasn't paying for those knockers on a waitress's salary, and even if she was, you don't get them that size unless you're in the sex industry."

"Maybe she got a loan," I said. "And maybe she got them that size because she liked them that size. Look, I work in sex crimes, okay? So I'm going to need you to get your brain out of the Dark Ages and stop making misogynistic assumptions about our victim."

"Meh." He sat back and flicked his cigarette ash out the window. "What does your girlfriend think about you working in sex crimes?"

"My girlfriend?" I looked at him. "I'm not gay."

"Oh, right."

"What made you think I was gay?"

He waved his cigarette at my head. "Your hair."

We pulled into an old apartment block in Auburn and parked in the visitors' space. I didn't talk to Tox on the way up the damp concrete steps. If he was going to make me this mad every time we spoke,

I was going to have a brain aneurysm before we actually discovered what had happened to Claudia Burrows.

Tox's sexism wasn't helped by Nigel Spader and his team rebuffing me from the Georges River Killer case. The Australian police force had always been full of boys' club antics, what Sam called the "ancient brotherhood bullshit." I was disappointed to see it creeping into my own station. Pops was a good chief, and didn't let even the most minor sexual harassment or favoritism play down between his staff. But I had the feeling Nigel and his boys didn't want me on the task force because I was a woman, and that even if Claudia did turn out to be one of the Georges River victims, they'd take the case off me completely. This was going to be a history-making case. There would be books about it. Nigel wanted his face on one of those books. He oozed heroic smugness.

Tox opened Claudia's door with the keys her parents had given us. He'd only prized it open a crack when it slammed back against him.

And someone inside yelled, "Go! *Go!*"

CHAPTER 16

HOPE ANALYZED HER reflection in the jewelry shop window, pulling the wig down slightly at the front and straightening her skirt-suit jacket. She'd kept only one of Jenny Spelling's suits in a hideous mustard yellow, the closest fit and the most modern piece she could find. It looked as though Jenny hadn't updated her wardrobe in decades. That irritated Hope. She couldn't stand people who'd been lucky enough to grow up in the lap of luxury who then refused to use the money they'd squirrelled away. She didn't know much about Jenny, but she couldn't understand how anyone respected her, dressed like this. She felt awkward in the slightly too-big heels, like a child playing dress-up.

Her first stop when she got the money was going to be shopping, for herself and for the boat. The *galley* needed new curtains, and the *bridge* needed a lamp. Hope tried to contain the excitement bubbling up inside her, taking a deep breath before she walked into the bank.

She went directly to the manager's desk and sat down on the chair there. A young man with a big Adam's apple came wandering out, his face spreading into a smile.

"How can I help you?"

"Oh, hi." Hope extended a hand. "I'm Jenny Spelling. I'd like to make a transaction from my savings account, please."

"Of course." The young man glanced towards the queue waiting at the counters. "Is this a large transaction?"

"I'd like to empty the account and close it, actually," Hope said. "Nothing to do with your bank. You've been wonderful to my husband and I, but we're moving overseas and we'll be starting a local account there."

"Well, congratulations!" the young man said. "What an exciting time. Let me just get your identification, Mrs. Spelling, and we'll have a look for you."

Hope opened Jenny Spelling's clunky leather wallet and extracted her driver's license and credit card. She kept a hand up near her eyes, playing with the edge of her low, heavy bangs, as the young man looked over the cards.

It worked. He went to the computer beside him and started tapping. Hope could feel sweat running down the backs of her calves. She squirmed in the older woman's shoes, trying to keep a straight face.

"So it's your main savings account that you'd like to close? Or would you like to close your everyday account as well?"

"Oh, all of it," she said. "I'll take all of it, please."

CHAPTER 17

HOPE GLANCED AT the screen and noted the amounts in the accounts. The everyday was petty cash, but the digits in the main savings account made her heart twist in her chest. So close to her dream. So close to everything she'd ever wanted. She needed to play it cool now. She touched her eyebrow as a muscle began to twitch there.

"Um, so it says heeeere…" The young man frowned and clicked. "Says here this is actually a joint signature account."

"What?" Hope choked.

"Right here." The young man turned the screen towards her, tapped its glossy surface. "When you and your husband opened the account, you made a provision that you could only extract more than a thousand dollars from this account if you both came into the bank and signed for it."

"Fuck!" Hope blurted. She covered her mouth. "I mean, oh, dear. Um."

"You don't remember making that provision?" the young man asked. Hope scratched at her throat. "No, I don't."

"Where did you open the account?"

He turned the screen back towards himself while Hope shifted in her chair.

"Oh, God, it was such a long time ago." She laughed. "Look, let me get a thousand dollars, and I'll get Ken down here to empty the main savings with me some other time."

"Right." The young man was looking at her very closely now. Hope turned her face away, glanced at the people waiting in line at the counter. "Would you like to empty the everyday as well? That account is yours alone."

"I know that," Hope snapped. She shoved her hands into her lap. "I'm sorry. Yes. I know that. I'll empty that account, too. Mmm-hmm."

The young man made some movements with his mouse. While he clicked and scrolled, Hope watched his face, until his eyes slid over and met hers.

"All right?"

"Yep." Hope smiled.

"All right." The young man got up and gave a cheerful smile. "I'll be back in just a minute."

Hope could hardly wait for him to count out the bills. She grabbed the money and her cards from the desktop and practically ran to the door.

In the street she paused and looked at the men and women passing by, their eyes on their phones. She'd hoped no one else would have to die for her plan to be completed. But something inside told her that more blood would be needed to wash away the life she was trapped in.

CHAPTER 18

I GOT OUT my gun and kicked in the door of Claudia's apartment, slamming it against the guy who'd just closed it on us. He fell into a coffee table covered in beer bottles, scattering them everywhere. There was another guy at the entrance to the kitchen. I pulled my gun up and shouted but he ran in there, hoping for an exit. There was none. Tox grabbed the first guy, picked him up out of the ruined coffee table and threw him into the television stand, crunching DVD boxes and splintering the screen of the cheap plasma. I went to the kitchen doorway and was narrowly missed by a flying frying pan. Two saucepans and a handful of cutlery came sailing out after it.

I put my gun away and grabbed the frying pan from the couch where it had landed. When I rushed into the kitchen the guy cowered into the corner near the blender as I wielded the pan above my head.

"How do you like it?" I yelled. His arm was raised against the weapon, eyes squeezed shut.

"Don't! Please! I'm sorry!"

I let him up.

"Shit, man! You're one crazy bitch!"

"Get out there." I yanked him towards the door. Tox had the other guy on the floor beside the glass heap that had been the coffee table.

Bright red blood was pouring down Tox's chin and neck, making a neat column on his chest.

"Little prick kicked me in the face." Tox looked at the blood on his hand.

"What are you dickheads doing here?" I kicked my guy along the floor until he was beside his friend. "You know Claudia Burrows is dead, right?"

"We heard about it." My guy was holding his head of black dreadlocks, his eyes welling with tears of panic. "She borrowed some money from our boss three weeks ago. We were told to come get it before the police swept in and took everything."

The intruders had gathered a small pile of cash and electronic goods and put them on the couch, with some jewelry clumped into a Chinese takeaway container.

"How much did she borrow?" Tox asked.

"Not much. Five grand. It was a short-term loan. She said she was coming into some big money and she'd get it right back to us."

"Shhh, dude." Tox's guy nudged his friend. "Fuck, man. Who you talkin' to?"

"Pfft, they don't care." Dreadlocks waved dismissively at me. "They just care who killed her."

"How did you hear she'd been killed? Her body was only found last night."

"My brother's a patrol cop in Newtown." Dreadlocks waved again.

"Your brother's a cop and you're a loan shark's bitch?" I snorted. "No guessing who got all the hugs."

"What did Claudia borrow the money for?" Tox asked. "Did she say?"

"We're not talking any more. That's it. We're done."

"All right, well, it's down to the station with both of you for breaking and entering." I took the cuffs off the back of my belt. "And maybe assaulting a police officer."

"She needed clothes!" Dreadlocks wailed as I dragged him up and threw him on the couch. "Good girl clothes."

"What do you mean, 'good girl clothes'?"

"Shut up, Ray! Fuck!"

I cuffed Ray and left him moaning in regret on the couch, his face pressed between the pillows. In the bedroom, Claudia's things had been thrown about, drawers emptied onto the bed and her jewelry tipped onto the floor. I went to the closet and pushed open the doors, and immediately I could see what Ray meant. Claudia's clothes were scant—tiny tops and tight leggings, plenty of sequins and beads and the odd strip of gold leather. I pulled out a complicated black corset of velvet, the buckles jangling as I set it on the bed.

At the very end of the closet, there were three new outfits hanging, long-sleeved silk blouses and pencil skirts in plastic sheaths. Beneath them on the carpet was a pair of brand-new sensible leather pumps. I checked the brands of the outfits, tugged a price tag that was still attached to one of them. Damn. These were certainly "good girl" clothes. Against the rest of her wardrobe, these outfits seemed like a disguise. I bent down as one of the jackets slid off the hanger and gathered it up from the floor, spotting a dusty white powder on the wrist. I gathered it up and tasted it, expecting cocaine, but I was surprised. It was dry salt. Slightly fishy-tasting. Sometime recently, Claudia had worn these clothes by the sea.

CHAPTER 19

I NEEDED COFFEE. All the calm and contentment I'd managed to generate last night by giving Ben Hammond a pounding was gone now. My shoulders were as hard as stone. We stopped at a café on the way back to the city and Tox dragged out an ancient black laptop.

"Claudia's parents said nothing about her being a hooker." I rubbed my eyes. "Maybe she was just dipping into the industry briefly to raise some money to go to college."

"So why borrow the five G's then?" Tox asked. "Why spend them on conservative clothes?"

"I don't know. But while we're on the subject of clothes, you'll need to change before we go much farther."

The waitress was so distracted by the blood on the front of Tox's shirt that she hardly managed to get our order down. My new partner's eyes were steadily blackening and there was a graze above his nasal bone. Tox glanced at his shirt.

"Eh," he said.

"You're going to go to college," I mused. "Start fresh. Make something of your life. You're twenty-four years old, so you've left it late, but not that late. You've been accepted. What do you do?"

"You go out and buy textbooks," Tox said.

"Right. Textbooks, a laptop maybe. Not expensive clothes. And where's this money coming from in the first place? The big money she says she's about to come into?"

An e-mail came up on my phone and I checked it. It was a brief summary from the medical examiner, a quick review of his initial findings before the full autopsy on Claudia Burrows. Tox had been right about the livor mortis, and the pulmonary edema, and the fact that Claudia had likely been dead a day, in the water about twenty hours. He was also right about the breast implants. I saw him smiling at his laptop screen. He'd probably just gotten the same e-mail.

"This is interesting," I said. "She'd had her hair dyed and cut no more than a week ago. And she'd taken a good bonk to the back of the head."

"Feet are showing blisters from the new high heels," Tox added.

"So whatever she needed to jazz up her appearance for, she's done it in the last week or so. Parents didn't mention any job interviews. Weird."

Our coffees came. I gulped mine and ordered another.

"'Skin slippage around the right ankle suggests ligature, ante-mortem, for a short amount of time, pulling downward over the front of the foot towards the toes,'" I read. "So she was weighed down when she went in the water."

"How do you figure that?"

"Well, weight goes into the water." I drew a circle on the greasy tabletop with my finger, a line rising from it. "Rope goes up from the weight, ties around Claudia's ankle. Claudia floats upward, pulling the rope down towards her toes. The rope doesn't bruise her too badly because it comes loose in the storm, letting her body float away."

We fell into silence to consider the images before us, the cold medical text detailing Claudia's horrific last moments on earth.

"This is a pretty nasty killer we have here," I said. "I can't imagine why throwing her in alive was necessary. By the time you've got her tied to the weight, she's under your control. Why not put her out of her misery? Why make her think about the journey down to the bottom of the sea? It's so vicious."

"I don't know about that," Tox said. "Think about it. Putting her out of her misery is extra effort. Extra *consideration*. What we might have here is someone who isn't even that thoughtful. Someone who never thought about what the victim would or wouldn't feel. I think we're looking for a killer whose priority is getting the job done, ticking the boxes. Just my opinion."

I pushed my phone away and studied his face as he checked through the rest of his e-mails. I couldn't help but feel an icy heaviness in my chest at his talk of priorities and getting the job done. He'd shown himself to be just that kind of man. Unconcerned with what people feel. I wondered if he was just talking about Claudia's victims, or his own ones, too.

CHAPTER 20

MY KNUCKLES STILL hurt from the impact against the back of Ben Hammond's skull, but I wasn't focusing on that as I smacked my opponent in his ribs, his chest. I surged forward and drove an elbow into the side of his padded head. Pops backed up into the corner of the ring. I didn't think of him as the old, squat man that he was. In the ring we were equals. I gave him a couple of jabs in the face and backed off to let him out of the trap he'd fallen into.

"Mind that back step." The Chief pointed at my foot with his red boxing glove. "Don't cross."

Pops had been training me since I'd arrived at Sydney Metro to take up the grand position of the only woman on the sex crimes squad. There hadn't been a female in my role for five years, but the department had wanted someone victims could relate to, someone who wouldn't accidentally intimidate them with their masculine hulk in the tiny station interview rooms. It wasn't long after arriving that I'd decided I needed some form of self-defense, my days filled with horrific stories of attacks in alleyways and empty parking lots, young girls ensnared walking home across darkened parks by fiendish predators. I was probably getting too swift for Chief Morris, who had been training boxers since before I was born. But I trusted his advice. He'd made me strong, and he didn't take less than full commitment in his sessions.

"Tell me about the Georges River case," I said, batting away his swing at my face. "Why were your guys so sure my girl wasn't one of the victims?"

I'd given up on the idea that Claudia Burrows was a Georges River Killer victim. But something was nibbling at me about the certainty with which Nigel had shoved me away. Nigel hadn't even been called to Claudia's crime scene for a look. How could they know their killer wasn't responsible?

"Have you guys got a suspect?" I asked.

"Leave it, Harry," he said.

"You must be pretty set on this suspect if you're certain he didn't kill Claudia," I said. "Maybe because you were watching your suspect when Claudia was killed. Am I right? Have you got enough for an arrest?"

"I didn't even say we had a suspect."

"Well, if you don't have a suspect, I have to assume you're letting Nigel and his band of asshats push me away because they want it to be a men-only case."

I punched Pops in the stomach. He fell against the ropes.

"Harry—"

"I'm a good cop, you know." I thumped my chest with my boxing glove. "Being a woman shouldn't exclude me from anything."

"No one's excluding you."

"The Camden strangler? Dennis Yama? David Paris, that cannibal guy? They were all me, Pops. Homicide got the credit, sure, but it was the sex crimes side of those investigations that put them on track."

"Harry, no one's doubting your abilities."

"Then why the fuck am I being shut out?"

I pummeled Pops with a series of hits to the head. Without warning, he clutched at his chest and fell into the corner of the ring. I watched in horror as he collapsed.

CHAPTER 21

"OH, SHIT!" I tore my gloves off. "Shit! Pops! I'm sorry!"

I dragged the old man to his feet. He unclipped the padded helmet and let it fall to the mat. His face was red and drenched in sweat. He thumped his chest as though he had heartburn and shook his head.

"Are you all right?"

"Yeah, yeah."

"I'm sorry. I got carried away."

"You're too good for your old trainer, Harry." He batted me on the shoulder with his glove. "You're a good cop, too. You're not being shut out of the Georges River task force because of your abilities, or your gender. You gotta let it go. Okay?"

"Why?" I followed the old man to the stool at the opposite corner of the ring. I handed him the bottle of water sitting there. "I just don't understand. I feel like there's something you're keeping from me. And we've never been like this, Pops. We've never kept things from each other."

The old man sucked at the water bottle and regained his breath. He wouldn't meet my eyes. I ducked my head to try to see what was hidden there, whether it was guilt or shame or concern cutting him off from me. But he wiped his forehead on the back of his arm and turned away.

"It'll all come out in time," he said. "And when it does, you'll...you'll be grateful for all the time you *didn't* know the truth."

CHAPTER 22

HOPE NEEDED TO stay calm. It was rational planning and control that was going to get her through this. As soon as she had the Spellings' money, she was out of here. Off towards the sunrise on the gentle waves. She'd never look back on Sydney, on the feast of horrors the city had provided over her life. This town deserved to burn. She walked along the pier between the yachts and looked at the glowing city towers reflected in the black harbor. Soon she'd be underway.

Her plan was to leave behind the memories of what she had done to Jenny and Ken Spelling, along with the memories of her father and his sweaty, grabby hands. She'd try to replace the night beast he'd become after her mother's death with the man she remembered from her early childhood, his eyes set on the horizon, one warm hand on hers as he taught her to direct the helm, taking them out towards the edge of forever. She'd leave them behind with the memories of her almost skeletal mother curled up in the tub she'd died in, with the smoke-saturated bedrooms of the Black Garter hotel where she'd worked for almost all of her adult life. If she closed her eyes, she could still see the red lamplight out the front of the house of horrors, the men smoking there, looking at their phones, talking about the girls inside and which ones provided which services. Soon, when she closed her eyes, it would be the Caribbean sun burning red light there. Or maybe Key Largo. She hadn't decided yet.

As she powered the *New Hope* east out over the South Pacific, she'd jettison the images that sometimes zapped through her. Claudia's howling mouth as she'd sailed downward into the blackness of the ocean, the anchor yanking her soundlessly into the dark. Her confused eyes as Hope had come into the kitchen after they'd secured the Spellings in the bathroom, the hammer in her fist.

I thought we were in this together....

Her squeal of disbelief as Hope had raised the hammer above her head.

CHAPTER 23

HOPE STILL CARRIED the hammer with her in Jenny's cream Louis Vuitton handbag. She supposed she'd have to get rid of that, too. She was dreaming as she wandered along mooring number 17 and almost ran into the overweight man with the clipboard standing there.

"Oh! Sorry!"

"It's all right." He laughed. His name tag said STEVE. "Is this your yacht here?"

"Yes, it is, actually." Hope smiled. "It's just come out of dry dock. I signed in at the office."

"Yes, yes, that's all good." Steve glanced at his clipboard. "I'm actually just doing a safety inspection. The coastguard makes us do spot checks now and then on all the moorings."

"Uh-huh." Hope chewed her lip. She listened to the boat beside them. Was that thumping she could hear? Could Steve hear it, too?

"Everything's fine. It's just…it's so weird." Steve pointed with his pen to a red cone-shaped device strapped to the side of the deck. "I'm running checks on all the EPIRBs to make sure they're all registered and up to date, and this one isn't right."

Hope shifted her handbag on her shoulder. "An EPIRB?"

"It's an emergency position-indicating radio beacon." Steve looked at the sky, recited the words carefully. "Ha, that's what I think it stands for, anyway. That beacon gets wet and it'll send a signal to the coastguard telling them you're in trouble. You'll want to chuck it in the water long before you start to sink, though!"

"Right." Hope laughed.

"They also kind of act like a microchip would in your family dog," Steve said. "They're registered to particular people, and particular boats, in case the boat gets lost. Or the people get lost! Ha! Now, I'm seeing that your boat here is the *New Hope*. But when I look up your EPIRB number on the computer, it says this boat should be *Dream Catcher*."

Steve tipped his clipboard, which he used to balance a thin computer tablet. Hope hardly glanced at the numbers on the screen.

"Did you change your vessel's name, Ms...." Steve looked at the screen. "Ms. Spelling?"

"Uh, no." Hope wiped sweat from her neck. "No, this is…this is a different vessel. That we…we only recently purchased, my husband and I."

"Oh."

"I mean, I'm not even Ms. Spelling." Hope drew a long breath. "Whoever that is. I'm…uh."

Steve waited.

"Look, would you like to come aboard?" Hope gestured to the yacht. "Come on board and I'll show you the paperwork and we can sort all this out."

"Sure thing." Steve smiled. He turned and stepped across the small gangway to the deck.

Hope followed, sliding her hand into the darkness of her handbag and around the polished handle of the hammer.

CHAPTER 24

DESPITE THE EVENING gym session, I couldn't sleep. I desperately needed to. I called my brother and blasted him with complaints about Tox as soon as he picked up.

"What actually *is* the story with this guy?" he said. "How can he possibly be a cop if you're saying he's killed two people?"

"No idea," I grunted. "People are saying he was seven years old. If I had to guess, I'd say that because of his age at the time of the crime, he'd have been charged with involuntary manslaughter, if he was charged with anything at all. Apparently it was a group of boys, not just him. So his lawyers would have said he was influenced by the group, and far too young to know what he was doing."

"But you don't actually know any details about it?"

"No, the records are sealed. I tried to have a look before I left work this afternoon."

Sam scoffed. "So it's all just rumor, really?"

"What are you getting at?"

"Maybe he didn't do it."

"If he didn't do it, he'd have set everyone straight, right?" I said. "The bosses would have set everyone straight. He must have done it."

We fell silent.

"I'd like to think he didn't do it," I admitted. "But when I look in his eyes, I'm not so sure."

CHAPTER 25

I SAT IN bed all night on the computer after speaking to Sam, clicking around, looking for Claudia Burrows. She'd recently scrubbed her social media presence clean. There were suggestions that she'd once had a Facebook page and a Twitter account, but these were empty now, the links broken. I saw a couple of pictures of her on sites that must have belonged to her friends. She was a very different girl from the one whom I'd seen washed up on the shores of the Georges River. Her hair, which had been short and dark when she died, was long and bleach-blond, the roots dark and the ends scraggly. I learned that she sometimes went under the name Claudia Dee. Did multiple names mean multiple identities? Was it Claudia Dee who'd worn the skimpy clothes that filled most of her wardrobe, and Claudia Burrows who'd bought the more formal attire?

I didn't like the idea that Claudia had been pretending to be someone else, and that she'd recently told her creditors that she was coming into money. Had she been conducting a scam? If so, who was the victim? Had she been planning a robbery? I put the laptop away, discouraged by all the dead ends, and tried to sleep. Ten minutes later I had it open again, doing different searches.

At midnight I called Chris Murray, the detective from the Surry Hills station.

"Do you have any idea what time it is?"

"Murray," I said, "you've got connections in the records department, don't you? I want you to help me out. I'm wandering aimlessly around the Internet looking for anything I can get on Tox Barnes. Maybe they changed his name after the crime? Is that why I can't find any newspaper articles about him?"

"The fact that you're carrying on working with that monster without looking for an out is exactly the reason I won't help you," he said. "You should be trying to get away from him, not trying to understand him. I'm hanging up, Harry."

"Murray, don't go! I need help here, man."

"He *murdered* a woman and her kid," Murray said. "He and a bunch of other kids stabbed them to death."

"I thought they beat them to death."

"Is how they did it very important?"

"I guess not. What exactly am I supposed to do, Murray? I've got a homicide on my hands. You know how often I get homicides in sex crimes? I can't just walk out on this."

"Feign sickness and leave the case to him," he said. "He's good at what he does. He'll solve it himself in no time. Probably uses his killer instincts."

"This is what people do?" I shook my head. "They just drop him?"

"He's like a curse. You either find some way to drop him or shuffle him onto someone else. Otherwise you'll look like you're on his side, and you don't want people thinking that, Harry."

"This is insane."

"He's a disgrace to the force," Murray said. "He's a disgrace to what we stand for as police."

"But wasn't he only seven years old when the crime occurred?"

"I got a six-year-old," Murray snapped. "She knows it's wrong to kill people. Hell, my three-year-old knows that. I'm too busy for this shit, Harry. I got a couple of missing yachties from Queensland on my desk. I'm looking at hundreds of pictures of identical boats all day long. I'm seein' boats in my fucking sleep."

"What are you doing with a Queensland case?"

"Oh." He sighed. The wind seemed to go out of him suddenly. "Long story. It's bad. It's just one of those ones that gives you the creeps."

"Tell me about it," I said. I hoped by listening kindly to his problems for a few minutes, he'd take his fury down a few notches. It seemed to work. When he spoke again, his voice was softer.

"A retired couple in their fifties was last seen on their yacht heading south out of Brisbane. They travel a lot, so the woman does her own kidney dialysis on the boat. She's got some kidney problem, I don't know what. But she hasn't filled her prescription for the dialysate—the stuff she rinses her kidney with. By the family's calculation, the couple should have dropped into Sydney a couple of days ago at the latest to fill the prescription. If they did drop in, they didn't sign into the marina, and they haven't filled the prescription. Nobody on the east coast has seen them. They were selling the boat. It's possible they swung in and picked up potential buyers. But we don't know."

"Jesus," I said, as sympathetically as I could. "Sounds complex. Why haven't I seen it getting much press?"

"It's early days yet. And these yachties go missing all the time. Decide to change direction on a whim and don't know their comms aren't working. Everybody's hoping they'll just pop up again in Indonesia or something. I don't know. I got a bad feeling about it. The coastguard is on the lookout."

"Anything I can do?"

"No, Harry, there's nothing you can do." His tone sharpened again, as though he'd realized I was only listening because I wanted his help.

"Look, Murray, I want to understand what I'm dealing with here," I pleaded. "What exactly is Tox supposed to have done? How many people were involved? I want to know exactly what he was charged with. I've got to find out what kind of man he is."

"I don't know, Harry, but I'm disgusted that you're even interested," Murray said. "We're supposed to be the good guys. He's an insult to us, and so are you right now."

The phone clicked dead in my ear.

CHAPTER 26

THE BLARING OF a horn woke me. When I looked out my bedroom window, Tox Barnes was sitting in the driver's seat of his black '69 Mustang, revving the engine. When I got in the car he tossed his phone into my lap.

"Check it out, zombie face," he said.

"'Zombie face'?"

He flipped the mirror down in front of me. He was right: I looked decidedly undead. I rubbed my eyes and raked back my apparently homosexual hair, slapping the mirror away.

On the phone screen was a video on pause. I clicked play, and the car was filled with the sound of deep-throated groaning and grunting.

"Urgh." I threw the phone back at him with barely a glimpse of the bare thrusting ass on the screen. "You're disgusting."

"I'm not sharing my porn with you. That's our victim, Claudia Burrows."

I took the phone back and watched. The camera panned around the ass and up the thighs of a petite blonde woman. I'd seen that mouth before, with Tox Barnes's finger in it.

"Where'd you find this?"

"I was trying to figure out how she got those tits," he said, pulling away from the curb. "Her bank account showed she'd never been able to afford them. Then I got to thinking—adult film producers will sometimes pay for larger hooters for their actresses if they agree to appear in a certain number of movies. The films sell better if the girls have got a set of big juicy—"

"All right, all right, all right."

"She appears in that video as Claudia Dee." He pointed with his cigarette. "Had an old porn addict I know dig it up for me. It's about a month old. Straight to DVD, not available online."

"Nice work."

"Maybe that's where the big payoff was coming from," he said, roaring through the traffic like a lunatic, weaving in and out of the oncoming cars. "Maybe there was a feature film coming up."

"Yeah, and maybe she pulled out of the big film," I said, "and someone decided they weren't going to be messed with like that. I've met plenty of these porn guys. Women are just like horses to them. When they break down, or they go wild, you take them out the back and put a bullet in their brains."

CHAPTER 27

DIABOLIC VIDEOS HAD a studio on the upper floor of a building on bustling George Street, up a flight of carpeted stairs that reeked of gasoline. A huge pink neon sign at the top of the stairs blinded me as I arrived at the tiny foyer where a girl with too many piercings sat texting.

"What is that smell?" I covered my mouth and nose with my T-shirt.

"Some girl's ex-boyfriend came in here last week lookin' for her." The pierced girl yawned. "Poured gasoline all down the stairs. Said he was gonna light the place on fire if she didn't come out."

"She come out?" Tox asked.

"The place on fire?"

"We're looking for people who know this girl here." I showed her a picture of Claudia her parents had provided us with. Piercings hardly glanced at it. She only had eyes for Tox.

"You don't look like no cop."

"What do I look like?"

"I dunno." The girl leaned on the counter, wriggled her booty. "But I like it."

"This! Girl! Here!" I slapped the photo on the counter.

"Okay! Okay! Jeez!"

She pushed aside a curtain and led us through. The space was divided into quarters by painted black partitions. I could hear whips cracking in the farthest corner. We passed an empty bed and arrived in the middle of a film set. Two huge black cameras were manned by men. On a satin-sheeted bed, an unnaturally hairless woman was propped, the hem of a blazing-white tennis skirt flipped back over her thighs. Her cotton polo shirt was ripped across the middle and tied tight beneath enormous breasts. She twirled a blond pigtail in one hand and licked the handle of a tennis racquet she held in the other.

Tox pointed. "What is she gonna do with that racquet?"

"Excuse me!" A man with a clipboard stepped out of the glow of the lights. "You're in the middle of a live shoot here!"

"I'm Detective Blue. This is Detective Dirtycreep. We're looking for someone who was close to Claudia Burrows." I flashed the picture. "We know she did a film here a couple of months ago. We want to speak to anyone who has any knowledge about her murder."

"I've never seen that girl before." The producer turned his nose up at the picture. "If she's dead, it's her own fault."

Someone tapped me on the shoulder and I turned around, only to be yanked face first into yet another pair of breasts. The girl hugging me was wearing six-inch silver sparkle heels, and nothing else.

"Harry!" she squealed. "Oh, my God, you little doll, what are you *doing* here?"

I'd handled Vicky Varouma's sexual assault claim at Surry Hills a couple of years earlier.

"Vicky!" I smiled up at her. "Hi! Tell me you know this girl."

"Oh, man." Vicky's face fell as she took in the picture. "Now there's a piece of bad news."

CHAPTER 28

"SHE WAS TALKING about everything changing," Vicky said. "She was outta here. She asked me for some money so she could get set up, and said she'd pay me back when she came into her big win."

"What was the money for?" I asked. We were sitting in the Diabolic Videos dressing room. I'd caught sight of myself in the mirror and realized Vicky's hug had covered my face and neck in body glitter. It was proving difficult to wipe off. Tox stood nearby, examining bottles of perfume.

"I don't know. But I saw her near Potts Point wearing some pretty flashy clothes. I was driving by and she was with another girl. Maybe she had a job or something."

"Who was the other girl?"

"I don't know that either. They were shopping for handbags. On *Macleay Street*. Damn, girl must've hit something good."

"Why did you say out there that Claudia was 'bad news'?" Tox asked.

"Oh." Vicky looked embarrassed, turned to the mirrors and started braiding her hair. "I feel bad now. She's dead. You shouldn't speak ill of the dead."

"You should if it'll help us."

"She was just a slimy character, our Claudia." Vicky sighed. "The kind of girls who end up in this industry aren't usually your silver spoon types. But I'd met Claudia's parents and they seemed like nice, quiet people. Regular people. I couldn't figure out how she ended up the way she was. So deceptive. She always had a scam on the go."

"Like what?"

"Oh, like she'd tell you she knew where to get cheap ecstasy or something, you know, for the weekend. She'd take your money and come back crying, telling you the dealer had robbed her, smacked her around. She'd show you bruises that were nonexistent, or days old. That sort of thing."

"Right."

"She lied like you wouldn't believe, so she made a good actress for Diabolic. I think her parents thought she was a waitress or something. But she lied about things that didn't matter. She exaggerated and exaggerated until you were basically being asked to believe she had this crazy, wild, extravagant life. She was dating movie stars and international spies."

"How sad," I said.

"She was always on the verge of a 'new life.' The big money she was supposed to be coming into? I don't know." Vicky shrugged. "Sounds like bullshit to me. I think she'd applied to the university. She was going to buy an apartment, transfer up into a law-school program, be a criminal lawyer. She kept watching clips from legal dramas on her phone, practicing them out loud. I mean, *please*—girl could barely read."

"How'd she get into school if she could barely read?"

"I'd say she had a friend fill in the application form for her. She'd have paid them to pack it full of lies about how she was ready to knuckle down and study." Vicky looked at me. "I can see why she was so determined to live a 'new life.' The life she was living here was a total fabrication."

CHAPTER 29

HOPE'S PLANS HAD stalled. She knelt on the deck of her yacht, sanding the scratches in the polished wood, trying to keep her fury contained. The scratches went all the way from the anchor mount to a door at the side of the vessel, from where she'd dragged the anchor she had tied Claudia to.

In the first days, Hope had been sick whenever she'd thought about it. All that would go in time. Already she couldn't remember her face. Piece by piece, the memories would fall away. She just had to continue with the plan.

Hope heard a shifting in the bathroom. She got up and marched there, slammed open the door. Finally he was awake. Ken was just coming to his senses, shaking the chloroform fog from his head. He looked down at his sleeping wife, at the sheen of sweat on her skin. The woman was ghost white.

"So I had a magnificent time at the bank," Hope snapped.

"You got the money?" Ken's eyes widened. "Now you can let us go. You can—"

"Don't pretend you didn't try to send me into a fucking trap, Ken." Hope slammed the door again so that it banged against the shower frame. "The joint signatures? You were hoping to trip me up, and your plan failed."

"I wasn't," Ken panted, swallowed hard. "Hope, look, I didn't try to betray you. I just want to get my wife to a hospital. I just want this to be over. Jenny has got hours, not days, until her kidneys are going to fail and she's going to die. Do you understand that?"

"Do you think I'm a fucking idiot?" Hope sneered.

"No." Ken shook his head. "No, of course not. You're very clever. It would take someone very clever to pull something like this off."

"I've planned every aspect of this thing," Hope said. "Nothing is going to stop me. I deserve this, you understand? I've waited my whole life for my moment. You've got to make your own life, Ken. You've got to change your own destiny. Nobody's gonna change it for you."

"Imagine if you staged an incredible plan like this without hurting anybody." Ken nodded along. "Wow! You'd show everybody. You'd go down in the history books."

Hope sighed. She'd been enjoying Ken's praise, but he'd taken it a step too far. The man must know what had happened to Claudia. Two young, professional women had approached him about his boat. Those same two had accompanied him and his wife around the harbor, followed him down into the engine cavity to inspect the boat's inner workings. Now that their real purpose had been revealed, one of those girls was gone. Even from the bathroom where she'd locked them, Ken and Jenny must have heard Claudia's scream as Hope had brought the hammer down on the back of her skull. The scrape of the anchor. She felt exhausted as Ken launched into his tired pleas again.

"It won't take long. All you have to do is bring the machine in here," Ken said. "There might be enough dialysate left for one more dose. Just untie one of my hands, and I'll—"

"You're going to die, Ken," Hope said suddenly. The man before her stiffened, his eyes wide. Hope shook her head, bored, as she continued: "You're both going to die. You might as well just accept that now."

CHAPTER 30

TOX AND I settled in a bar on the strip in Kings Cross, sitting at the open window, watching the pimps and prostitutes wander up and down in the light rain. It seemed appropriate to head into Sydney's red-light district. What we'd learned of Claudia's life made me gravitate here, where the liars, cheats, and criminals came to play. The homeless crowding into corners to escape the wind and the hopeless slouching around the bars, tired from weeks of endlessly drinking away reality. Kings Cross was also just around the corner from my apartment. I hoped to wander back after a quick drink and get some much-needed sleep.

My phone calls and e-mails were ceasing to have any effect as word spread throughout the police force that I was working with Tox. When I called to see if the full autopsy on Claudia's body had come in, an officer at my station put me on hold for half an hour, and then hung up. I only got the report by calling back and pretending to be someone else. I couldn't get hold of the secondary detectives I'd tasked to look after the Burrowses, so I called their lawyer and asked if everyone was okay. I stared at Tox while I waited on the phone, trying to decide how the man himself ever got anything done without fabricating multiple identities and ringing around the world every time he wanted anything.

While I watched, I found myself trying to imagine him as a small child in a wild pack of other kids, pulling and grabbing and yanking an adult mother to the ground, stabbing her in a hurried rush, blood soaking their tiny clothes. I imagined him cornering her son, a boy his age maybe, holding the knife to the kid's throat. Why had they done it? Tox had a mean look to him, particularly with the bruised nose and double black eyes, the leather jacket that reeked of smoke. But I knew there was no "killer look." I'd known baby-faced preteen boys in school blazers and caps who'd assaulted girls so viciously they'd broken their victims' spirits for life.

Maybe it was all just a rumor and Tox was innocent. But if it was, why didn't he do anything to change the black mark against his name?

I was just starting to imagine him as a kind and gentle man wrapped in the shell of a dangerous one when he put his whisky glass down, got up, and strode across the room with violent intent. I watched him take a pool cue from the rack, snap it over his knee, and roll the heavy end in his fist like a batter coming up to the plate.

"All right, buddy," he said, "let's go."

His target was a heavier, taller man who'd been playing a game of pool by the back doors of the bar. The heavy man and Tox lunged at each other.

CHAPTER 31

I WAS UP and across the bar before I'd really taken stock of the situation. My sheer bewilderment at the fight, and my own fatigue, had me diving into danger without a plan. I ran over and grabbed at Tox, but one of the heavy man's mates pulled me off him and threw me into the edge of the pool table. That hurt. My fists came up immediately, and I gave the guy a couple of warning punches to the jaw. But that only made him madder. He swung a heavy fist at my head. I ducked, surged up with an uppercut that crunched teeth and bone, and knocked him out on his feet. Before he could fall forward onto me, I shoved him back. He fell into a table full of glasses where two old men were seated. They hardly moved.

The room was suddenly full of people. I felt a hand on the back of my head, grabbed and twisted it, heard a man scream. I kicked his knee out and he flopped to the floor. I looked up just in time to see another fist swinging at me. It glanced off my brow. I ducked too late and shot the guy with a sucker punch to the gut that folded him in half.

Tox was holding his own against the guy he'd targeted originally. It looked as though it was all about to be over when five uniformed officers burst into the room, one of them leading a huge German shepherd on a leash.

"On the ground! On the ground!"

I flattened against the stinking carpet. The dog was standing right over me, barking in my face, slobbering in my hair. I realized I'd left my police-issue phone on the counter by the window when I'd run in to assist in the fight. As I lay being cuffed I saw a homeless man shuffle along to the window, pick up the phone, and continue shuffling.

We were dragged to a police van, which had been parked hastily on the street outside the pub. It was really raining now. Tox and I were shoved into the back of the van while the other fighters were herded up against the wall of the pub for a lecture about public brawls.

The lead patrol officer stood in the doorway and wrestled the keys into the lock on the van door.

"We're cops," I said. "We're both cops."

"We know," he replied, and slammed the door.

CHAPTER 32

WE SAT IN silence for a long time while the Kings Cross patrol cops drove us out of the city. Tox seemed genuinely unconcerned with our situation. He leaned back against the wall of the vehicle, watching me calmly as I worked through several levels of blinding rage.

"What the hell brought that on?" I asked eventually.

"We were in the academy together. Think he left the force a few years ago. He spotted me when we walked in. Started giving me the stink-eye. I thought he probably wanted a fight. So. You know." He shrugged.

"My life is becoming more difficult by the minute because of you," I snapped. "I can't even get people to answer the phone anymore. Now you've pulled this shit and I've lost my phone altogether."

"Meh. They'll issue you a new one," he rasped.

"Maybe!" I shrugged. "Maybe they'll just ignore me!"

"I'm hard to work with." Tox shifted, his cuffs clunking on the metal bench. "You must've guessed that."

"Well, I didn't know it'd be *this* bad."

"No one's forcing you to continue."

"Are you *kidding?*" I shook my head. "I'm supposed to drop the case completely because you're a murderer? This was my case to begin with, asshole!"

"You need to calm down," he said. "You're going all pink."

I tried to hold my tongue, but I was mad, and when I'm mad the words tumble out. If I get mad enough I start swinging. I was already imagining giving him a bop on that nose just to remind him how inconvenient he was.

"Did you do it?" I blurted, shifting to the edge of my seat. "Did you kill that mother and child?"

He looked up and held my gaze. "Yes," he answered.

CHAPTER 33

"WHY?" I ASKED.

Tox just looked at me. I wasn't going to get an answer that easy.

I shifted against the wall and sighed, let the rumble of the van rock me back into tired numbness. We seemed to be driving for an hour. I got up and tried to look through the slats in the door and figure out where we were.

"Where are they taking us?" I wondered.

"Not the Kings Cross police station," Tox said.

"Of course not the Kings Cross police station!" I sneered at him, fell into whining. "God, I should be in bed asleep now. I should have had a nice hot shower. I should have my lovely soft pajamas on."

"Pajamas?" Tox snorted.

The van stopped. I looked out the slats but could only see darkness, the occasional orange light. Two officers came around the back of the van and opened the door.

"Get out."

"I can't get down there with my hands cuffed behind my back."

"Get. Out."

I noted the names on their badges—Demper and Loris—and then gave up and let them have what they wanted, the humiliation they thought would make them feel like heroes. I made a jump for the ground, landed badly, and fell on my face. It sounded as if Tox didn't fare much better. I heard him slump onto his backside, try to slide off the edge and stumble.

One of the cops dragged me up. I'd bitten my lip. My mouth was full of blood. I sat on the ground as instructed, next to my partner. I was just getting an idea of where we were—some sort of industrial area near a canal—when blinding torchlight flashed in my face.

"Obviously you have no idea who this is." The cop flicked the light from my face to Tox's. My vision was clouded with green explosions.

"It's Tox Barnes," I said. "I'm well aware."

"Well, clearly you need an information session on who you're working with here, because you couldn't possibly know who he is—or you wouldn't be hanging out in bars with him. No one with any self-respect would," the cop carried on.

I sighed. Tox was squinting into the torchlight with one eye open. The light flicked between us, blinding us over and over.

"Tox Barnes and a few of his friends beat a woman and her young son to death."

"I know! I know!"

"Aren't you in sex crimes?" The second cop jabbed me in the shoulder with his boot, causing me to topple over. "How could you dismiss the gang rape and vicious beating of an innocent—"

I looked at Tox, thinking he'd jump in and correct an accusation as outlandish as this. He hardly seemed to be listening.

"Gang rape, too, now?" I struggled upright and squinted at the cop before me. I felt strangely defiant on Tox's behalf. "I can't keep up with all the versions of this story. What's next? Cannibalism?"

"She's on his side," one of them sneered. "I can't believe it."

"Where's your badge?"

"What?"

"Where's your fucking badge, bitch?"

I was shoved to the ground. The cop took my wallet from my back pocket and tore out the detective's badge. They took my cuffs off my belt, and my gun, too. Tox, they left alone. He watched, passive, from the dark beside me.

"You're an embarrassment to the force," the cop said, giving me a good kick in the ribs. He uncuffed me roughly and shoved my head into the dirt. "Have some dignity and leave this vicious dog alone."

They left us there in the dark, miles from the road.

CHAPTER 34

KEN SPELLING WASN'T going to die, not at the very moment he and his wife were beginning to settle into their well-deserved retirement. He was not going to die at the hands of some psychopathic freak who wanted to trade out of her shitty life the easy way.

Convincing her not to chloroform him had been easy—he'd simply not responded when she'd called from the doorway, having feigned a sluggish fever from around midnight. When he was sure Hope had left the vessel, he went to work. Ken kicked off his shoes and wriggled out of his socks. He stood in the middle of the tiny bathroom cubicle and stared down at his sleeping wife, trying to think of a plan. Jenny was sleeping for longer and longer periods now, and when she was awake she didn't make sense, her words slurred and delirious, her eyes unable to settle. Ken needed to act now, before it was too late. He took a deep breath.

All right, the door. That was a dead end. Though the bulkhead had wheels on either side, he'd heard Hope looping a rope through her side of the door every time she'd left them, probably tying it off against a pipe to lock them in. He experimented, turning his back to the door and shoving the wheel sideways with his bound hands. The wheel turned an inch or so and then clunked into place. Ken went to the wall beside the shower and kicked, listening to the sound ripple up through the iron hull. Yes, maybe he could signal someone by kicking. He lay on his back and kicked madly. Jenny barely stirred. In ten minutes he was drenched in sweat. He stopped and listened. There was not a sound from outside the vessel. He panted and stared at the ceiling of his prison.

Maybe if he kicked in a rhythm. Three fast, loud kicks, three slow ones, and three quick again. SOS. There had to be dozens of yachties wandering back and forth along the piers outside. Surely one of them would hear his signal.

But how long would Hope be gone? How long could he wait for his signal to be heard? Ken wasn't even sure all his racket was making it through the double hull of the boat to the outside world.

He stood again and looked at the porthole high on the wall behind the toilet. It had a single eye screw holding it shut. There was no way he could get it open with his hands tied. Or could he? Ken looked around the tiny room and spied the mop standing against the shelves of toiletries.

I'm not going to die, he thought. *I refuse to.*

CHAPTER 35

MY MAJOR BREAK came at midnight, but I ignored it. I was trudging up the stairs to my apartment block, scratching dried glitter and blood off my neck and trying to remember which key unlocked my front door. I'd lost my phone, but upstairs in my apartment I could hear the sound of my laptop jangling with a phone call. The ringing was finished by the time I reached the apartment. I ignored it and fell face down onto the couch.

I'd walked away from Tox in the dark of the industrial area without saying anything about the trouble he'd gotten us into. In truth, I was more horrified by his admission in the back of the van than I was by the roughhousing those idiot patrol cops had given us. It had taken fifteen minutes to find my wallet in the dark, up against the side of one of the warehouses where the officer had thrown it, and an hour to walk back to a major road. I'd stood there waiting for a cab for another half an hour, then had slept all the way home in it.

The laptop jangled again. I didn't know how long I'd been out. I crawled to the screen and tapped.

"What?"

"Harry? Vicky."

"Yep."

"I was telling someone here what happened to Claudia and I might have a lead for you," she said. I fumbled blindly in the dark across the cluttered coffee table for a pen. "One of the other girls said Claudia had been hanging around a prostitute from the Cross named Hope."

"Huh." I laughed. My instincts about Kings Cross and its connection to this case were right. The Cross was where dreams, lives, and promises failed. Claudia had been cooking up some kind of dream, and it had gotten her drowned at the bottom of the ocean.

"'Hope,'" I said. "That's all you got?"

"That's all I got."

"I'll take it. Thanks."

Almost immediately, an instant chat message popped up on the screen from my brother, wondering why I hadn't been answering my phone all night. I gave him a brief rundown of my experience out in the sticks, my fingers dancing over the keys.

SamBluDesigner77: Are you OK? Should you go to a hospital?

BlueHarry: I'm fine. It was just a roughhousing. No worse than the guys used to give each other at the academy.

SamBluDesigner77: You should report those cops! Not only is it assault, but if they didn't arrest you, dragging you out there against your will was probably abduction, right?

BlueHarry: You don't rat on your colleagues in this business, Sam. No matter what they do. We deal with our problems in-house.

SamBluDesigner77: God, it's all so pathetic.

BlueHarry: Speaking of abductions, how'd the second interview on the Georges River Killer thing go? What did they ask you?

I watched the screen for an indication that Sam was writing back to me. He started, and then mysteriously the speech bubble he was writing in disappeared. I waited for whatever was distracting him to go away, but he didn't start typing again. I had a strange urge to call him. My sisterly senses were in overdrive, but I told myself it was just fatigue.

CHAPTER 36

TOX DIDN'T HAVE any kind of desk. No police station would officially lay claim to him, so he would wander from station to station picking up cases as he liked. I'd heard his old department over in Auburn had started processing a transfer to North Sydney for him, and then the paperwork had "stalled." They'd been waiting for the police officer in the transfer position in North Sydney to transfer out, apparently, and then he hadn't. They'd filled Tox's spot in Auburn. So he existed in administrative limbo, not really Auburn's problem, not really North Sydney's. He might have complained and had the whole thing cleared up, but I got the sense that the wandering life suited him. He was basically a freelance detective, a consultant, but without the extra pay consulting detectives receive. Sometimes he would nab cases from the police scanner radio that he kept in his car. That's how he'd gotten onto Claudia's crime scene before me. He'd been out driving and had heard about the find.

When I arrived at Surry Hills station he was perched on the corner of one of the coffee-room tables, tapping away at that old, broken laptop. A group of my colleagues glared at the back of his head. I wondered if he'd gone home at all—he was still wearing the bloodied shirt. He didn't see me come in. Chris Murray was scrolling through pictures of boats. His computer screen was littered with CCTV footage of yachts. He looked at me guiltily as I went right to Pops's office and threw open the door.

"I need a gun, a badge, some handcuffs, and a phone," I said.

Pops glanced up. Detective Nigel Spader, whom I hadn't noticed sitting in the chair behind the door, burst out laughing.

"Oh, yeah," I said, slumping into the chair next to him. "It's really funny when police-issue items go missing. It's hilarious. Laugh it up."

"How did this happen?" Pops asked.

"How do you think? I'm radioactive from spending too much time with Tox Barnes. I'm practically glowing. Cops are coming out of the woodwork to mess with me."

"Who?" Pops asked. "Which cops?"

I sighed. Pops knew I'd never snitch.

"No one's forcing you to stay with him." Nigel shrugged. "Just drop him. He'll solve it himself. There's a new sexual assault on the case board this morning. Tell him you've got to prioritize that."

I closed my eyes and reveled in a private fantasy in which I thumped Nigel's head back into the wall behind him.

"Maybe I should just drop him," I said. "Maybe I'll give the sexual assault to one of the probationary detectives and jump over onto the Georges River task force. Oh, wait! I forgot! I don't have a penis!"

Nigel sighed.

"Did you seriously shut me out of that case because I'm a woman?" I asked. "Or do you actually have a reasonable motive? Like, do you have a suspect? Why don't you think you can trust me with your suspect?"

Both men were quiet. Again I felt that strange tingling up the back of my neck that told me something was very wrong here. That there was something very important being hidden from me. But one look at Nigel's face convinced me it was just him and his team being misogynistic assholes. He looked like one.

Soon I would know how wrong I was.

CHAPTER 37

IT TOOK FIVE minutes just to get the mop across the room, shuffling the thing with his knees and feet, knocking it against the walls, the shower cubicle, his sleeping wife. Another hour to get the handle through the screw loop over and over, turning the screw just a quarter-inch at a time. He sat triumphantly in the middle of the tiny room, exhausted, looking at the porthole propped open with the mop, the glorious blue sky outside. His face had swollen with pressure around the duct tape gag, sweat pouring down his neck. He tried to rouse Jenny. If he could get her to wake, try to slip her smaller gag off by rubbing her face against the frame of the shower, shout for help out the porthole. She woke briefly, blinked at him with uncomprehending, bloodshot eyes. No. It was up to Ken to save them both.

The big man stood, steeled himself, and climbed up onto the toilet seat. He looked outside and saw no one. Never mind. There might be people only yards away, out of view. He got down and kicked the second shelf of the cupboard down. Jenny's bathroom products scattered everywhere. Perfume bottles shattered. Shampoo and moisturizer and toner, all manner of women's things. Ken grabbed a shampoo bottle awkwardly by the neck between his big and second toes and hopped over to the toilet, almost losing his balance and falling by the shower. He climbed up, and with an agonizing stretch of groin and hip and thigh muscles he didn't know he still possessed, he leaned against the shower, raised one leg, and slid the shampoo bottle through the porthole.

He heard the gentle splash. Looked outside and saw no one. Ken hopped down, shuffled to the pile of toiletries, and grabbed another bottle with his toes. He had to work as fast as he could. He wanted a steady stream of floating debris, more than the usual marina junk. Someone would spot his breadcrumb trail. Someone would rescue them before Hope got back from wherever she was.

It was their only chance of survival.

CHAPTER 38

IT TOOK SOME serious cage-rattling through the strip clubs, bars, and brothels of Kings Cross to hunt down information on Hope. I heard fragments of her tale from homeless girls lounging in the back doorways of the supermarkets and kebab shops there. She was whispered about by conspiratorial old men in the upper rooms of Pussy Cats, Showgirls, and Porky's, where the rubber stairs glowed all day long with neon lights.

A crowlike old madam on Ward Avenue with a split lip told us her full name—Hope Stallwood—and where she'd been staying. But like most working girls, Hope moved around a lot. She pissed off her roommates with her drinking and drugs and her loud, late-night entrances. She was always broke, downtrodden, sullen, tired.

I'd known plenty of girls like Hope in my time on the sex crimes squad. Mostly they ended up dead in a bed somewhere, and I was brought in to assess whether they'd been taken advantage of before they expired. They all looked the same after a while. Bruised thighs tangled in the dirty sheets.

Tox and I didn't talk about the night before. But I'd stopped viewing our relationship with any kind of hope that it might be extended a minute longer than it had to be. When this case was over, I was getting the hell away from him. It wasn't the ill-treatment I was suffering from my colleagues that disturbed me. It was the calm and gentle way in which he'd said "Yes" when I'd asked him if he was a killer. I replayed it in my mind, over and over, whenever I looked at him.

Yes. Yes. Yes.

It hadn't seemed possible that a man who'd done what he was supposed to have done as a child could be so normal. Well, normal-ish. I realized that I hadn't really believed he'd done it at the start. I felt shaken now that I could be so wrong about someone.

I followed behind him, lost in my thoughts as we moved from bar to bar and brothel to brothel. Everyone we spoke to about Hope Stallwood told us she was coming into money. Just like Claudia, she'd been on the verge of having it all.

I wondered if that meant we'd find her dead.

CHAPTER 39

WHEN HOPE GOT to Pier 14, she spotted two men standing by the edge looking into the water below them. Something about their fixed stare made her blood run cold. She walked by quickly and hazarded a glance at the gentle waves below, where a shampoo bottle and four other bottles floated.

"Where's it all coming from?" one of the men was saying. Hope looked, and saw he had a wet deodorant can in one hand and a bottle of styling mousse in the other.

"Let's go have a wander around," the taller man said. "See if we can see who's dumping rubbish."

"Oh, my God," Hope gushed, setting down her bag. "I'm so stupid. Those are mine."

The two men turned and stared at her. She took the bottles from the shorter man and shoved them into her bag. "I was cleaning out my bathroom this afternoon. I must have left the tub of products on the edge of my boat. Oh, this is so embarrassing. It must have fallen in."

"There's stuff everywhere," the tall man said, his face softening. "Couple of bottles floated over there, near Pier Sixteen."

"I saw a toothbrush." The shorter man laughed.

"God." Hope sighed dramatically and pushed her hair back. "God-damn it. I'll clean it all up, I swear. This is so embarrassing."

She hustled away towards the *New Hope,* glancing back to see the men laughing and muttering to themselves. Hope's eyes were burning in her skull. If she didn't need Ken so badly right now, his end might have come much sooner and bloodier than she'd planned.

CHAPTER 40

AN OLD INDIAN woman answered the door to Hope's apartment. She was even shorter than me, and peered out angrily from the crack in the door. When she saw Tox, she started to close it again. My boot was in the way.

"We're lookin' for Hope Stallwood."

"What do you want? The drugs!" the woman howled. "The drugs, they ruin all of you! She's not here. That whore! She took her drugs and she's gone!"

Tox shoved the door open, almost knocking the woman over. We found ourselves in a tiny, filthy kitchen. My boots stuck to the linoleum.

"I'll call the police!"

"*We're* the police," I said. "Sit down. Tell us where Hope went."

"You're the pimps! Pimps with the drugs! Rotten drug dealers! I'll call the police!"

A young couple had appeared in the doorway to a short hall. I walked past them into a labyrinth of tight rooms divided into smaller rooms by hanging sheets. There were mattresses on the floor everywhere. Aluminum foil on the windows. Everything reeked of cigarette smoke and curry powder. A baby cried somewhere. I stepped on someone's foot and apologized. The owner of the foot was sleeping and hardly noticed.

I didn't know how people lived like this. Prisons were better. There was black mold on the bathroom ceiling that could have been an inch thick. My mind was rushing with crimes as I looked around the ground. Possession of heroin. Possession of marijuana. Child endangerment. Child neglect. Rental fraud. Underage drinking.

Tox pushed aside a pair of damp towels and found a filthy, bare mattress in the corner beneath a window.

"Hope Stallwood was here?" he asked the young couple, who'd started following us around the apartment like wary dogs. They nodded.

Hope was long gone, but she'd left a couple of things behind. A plastic container of hair ties, some underpants and clothes that reeked of body odor, a few old, stiff pairs of shoes. I picked up a magazine and let it fall open. *Yachting Today*. There were yachts circled in the For Sale section of the magazine, the pages indented with scrawled red pen.

"What's this?" I showed Tox the circled boats. Was Hope lying here at night under the lamplight circling boats she dreamed of owning? Was it all fantasy, or was she actually making plans?

I held the paper close to my nose. She'd actually underlined some of the phone numbers for making inquiries. There were digits listed on the back page. I flipped forward a few pages and found a page was torn from the magazine. I ran my fingers along the ragged seam.

Tox and I realized what we were seeing at almost exactly the same moment. Goosebumps raced along my arms.

"We could call the magazine." He took out his phone. "Confirm which boat is missing from the mag."

"No," I said. "I know which boat it is."

CHAPTER 41

THIS TIME, SHE'D chosen the branch at Martin Place. The streets were flush with lawyers on their lunch hour gliding around in their slick suits. As their cab drove through the traffic towards their stop, Hope kept the gun pressed against the inside of the handbag in her lap, the barrel pointed right at Ken. She had to keep the fury in her heart contained now. This was the most important part of her plan.

The man beside her sat crumpled against the side of the cab. She might have broken a couple of ribs when she came at him with the hammer after his stunt with the toiletries. She didn't care. He deserved it. He looked pathetic sitting there, his eyes wandering over the people in the street. She could see on his face the desire to open the door and grab one of them, inform them that he was a hostage. His mouth fell open as the cab came to a stop at a set of traffic lights, right beside a police cruiser. Hope jiggled the handbag, reminding him of his situation.

"Try anything, anything at all, and I'll be right back on that boat with your wife before you can utter a sound," Hope murmured, glancing at the cabbie's face in the rearview mirror. "I'll shoot you, and before the police can work out where you've been, Jenny will be dead."

"I'm not going to try anything," Ken whispered. "You can take the money. Take everything. Just hold up your end of the deal and leave Jenny on the pier unharmed."

"We'll see if your performance is convincing enough," Hope said. "I'm not making any promises."

They walked to the manager's counter, arm in arm. She shot him the loving look of a happy wife, slid her hand down and gripped his rough, warm hand.

What a lovely creature he was. She almost didn't want him to die.

The manager this time was an older, portly Asian man in a nicely tailored gray suit. He wore a small pink flower in his lapel and stuck his hand out for a shake a good ten feet away from Ken.

"Sir, madam. How can I help you today?"

They explained their business. The manager wore genuine regret on his face that they would no longer be customers, but brightened again when they spoke of their plans to travel the Greek Islands. He waved them into his small private office as though he were welcoming them inside his own home.

"So." He eased into his chair and turned the computer monitor towards himself. The nameplate on his desk read "Bai Yim." "What's the approximate amount of your holdings here, Mr. Spelling?"

"Eight hundred thousand," Hope answered for him. She felt a pulse of electricity run through her phoney husband's body. Yes, Hope had seen their accounts, she just hadn't been able to access them. He must have been surprised at how far her planning went. He had no idea.

"So I imagine you'd like the amount in a direct transfer check?"

"No, we'd like cash."

"You're not concerned about carrying that amount of money overseas? International piracy is a real threat, you know."

"Oh, no, we've taken provisions." Hope smiled. "And we've got customs approval to take the amount out of Australia in cash, forgoing the ten-thousand-dollar limit."

Ken glanced at her. She was prepared. *Of course I'm fucking prepared,* Hope thought. *This is my one shot. I'm not going back to that life. I'm never, never going back.*

She pushed aside the flurry of images that swirled through her at the thought. Sweat-stained beds and needles. The crush and roar of the crowd on the strip. The hollering and laughing of men in the hallways. Money in, money out, money in, money out.

"I'll get our guard to escort you to your car, then," Yim said. "You can never be too careful!"

They all laughed. Hope put Jenny and Ken Spelling's IDs on the table. Mr. Yim hardly glanced at the cards. His eyes were on the computer screen as he tapped their names and numbers into the keyboard.

His expression changed in an instant.

CHAPTER 42

MR. YIM RUBBED his nose, glanced at Hope and Ken, and painted on a crooked smile.

"Everything seems to be in order." He rose unevenly from his chair. "I'll just—"

Hope grabbed the computer monitor and swung it towards her. The screen was blinking with a bright-red warning sign. She'd seen it reflected in the shiny buttons on the front of Yim's shirt, the light making the mother-of-pearl surfaces flash pink: NEW SOUTH WALES STATE POLICE ALERT.

There was a phone number, a brief message. Hope stood and whipped the gun out of her handbag. Yim threw his hands up.

"Did you press the button?"

"I—"

"Did you press the fucking button?" She actioned the pistol. Yim shook his head, but there was no telling if he was lying. She hadn't seen his hand move while he was sitting, but he could easily have nudged the silent alarm under the table with his knee. She'd seen him shift awkwardly in the chair before rising.

Time to initiate Plan B.

She turned and shot Ken twice in the stomach.

The man bucked violently at the impact, then doubled over. He didn't make a sound. Nor did the gun, thanks to the silencer. Hope shifted her aim to Yim, and the old man whimpered.

CHAPTER 43

HOPE WALKED STIFFLY towards the entrance, the gun tucked beneath her flowing silk shirt. The glass doors of the bank were only yards away, still opening and closing as people walked in and out. The silent alarm had not been tripped, or the doors would have slammed shut immediately, the bulletproof screens at the crowded counters flying up to the ceiling.

It was too late now to hope of getting the Spellings' savings. She'd have to settle for the yacht. If she could get into international waters before the police figured out where she was, she'd be fine. There would always be other couples to scam. Right now she was in flight mode. All that mattered was getting away.

She walked across the bank foyer to the doors. Hope didn't count on Ken's blood having run so quickly from his wounds in Yim's office. As Hope walked towards freedom, her stolen high heels left a series of red triangles in her wake on the huge white marble tiles. Hope looked up just as the teller at the end of the row noticed them, her frown deepening as she tried to work out how the customer could have walked in red paint inside the bank.

The two women's eyes met just as Hope reached the door.

"Excuse me, miss," the teller called. "Miss!"

Hope turned and ran.

She fitted through the glass doors as they snapped shut just at the last second, the edges catching her shirt, tearing the soft fabric. The crowd parted as she waved the gun in the air.

"Get out of the way! Move!"

There was a taxi on the corner. Perfect timing. Hope was going to make it through this. She was going to see that sunrise on the ocean. No one was going to stop her.

CHAPTER 44

ON THE WAY back to the station, stopped at the traffic lights at Elizabeth Street, three patrol cars zipped through the red signal in front of us, sirens blaring. An ambulance was hot on their tail. They were heading towards Martin Place at an incredible speed. I'd been trying to get Chris Murray on the phone, but he wouldn't answer. Finally I took Tox's phone and dialed, hoping Murray wouldn't recognize the number.

"Chris Murray."

"Murray, you asshole," I said, "you've been ignoring my calls!"

"I don't have time for your calls," he snapped back.

We yelled into the phone at the same time: *"I've found the yachties!"*

We were both panting with excitement, struggling through the confusion.

"What?" Chris said.

"I've—found—the missing couple," I stammered. "Well, I know who knows where they are. I'm tailing a suspect, a prostitute named Hope Stallwood, in my drowning case. I think Hope and my victim, Claudia Burrows, were working together to steal your couple's boat. Claudia ended up as excess baggage, maybe got dumped when the scam was over. Probably your yachties, too."

"Well, I'm hoping you're wrong about that," Murray said. "Because a young Caucasian female has just tried to access the couple's bank account in Martin Place. And they tell me that whoever she is, she wasn't alone."

"Jesus Christ! That must be her!"

"I'm on my way right now," Murray said.

"I'll see you there." I grabbed Tox just as we set off across the lights. "Turn the car around," I told him. "Head back towards Martin Place."

CHAPTER 45

WE RAN ACROSS the crowded square and pushed through the ring of people at the police tape around the bank. The alarms inside were still squealing, but the big glass doors were open and cops were running in and out. One passed me with his hands covered in blood, rubbing them on the front of his shirt, looking dazed.

I knew Hope was on the edge. Anyone who had lived for long enough in the kind of environment she had was probably pretty close to manic-depressive.

I spend so much of my job hoping I'm wrong. I hoped, as I pushed through the crowd, that somehow I'd made a mistake while joining the dots. Connecting the yachting magazine to the missing couple who had disappeared at sea. Maybe I was jumping to conclusions— leaping down a rabbit hole that would take me nowhere. I hoped I'd walk into the bank manager's office and find the missing couple there, safe.

I wasn't so lucky.

There was a man in his fifties on his back on the marble floor, bleeding to death in a huddle of paramedics. He'd been shot or stabbed, it looked like. The situation was so desperate that the paramedics had forgone getting him to the hospital and were trying to stem the bleeding right there, in front of everyone. There were female bank tellers in snappy red suits crying in each other's arms. I grabbed one and yanked her away from the tearful huddle.

"Who is he?"

"I don't know." She wiped her running mascara. "He came in with her, the shooter. They were a couple. Mr. Yim saw them in the office. We didn't hear the gunshots. They walked in together, and then she walked out. Someone saw blood and went in and found them."

I turned the corner and glanced into Yim's office. He was slumped against the back wall, his face gray, a bullet hole in his neck. Two men were holding a dark jacket against his wounds. But it was clearly over.

I heard the man on the ground struggling against the paramedics assisting him.

"She's still on board!" he cried, taking gasps of breath. "She's got her! She's got my wife!"

CHAPTER 46

HOPE LEANED AGAINST the bridge wall and kept the gun on Jenny, watched out the windows as the other yachties lounged and talked on their own vessels. Soon the cops would swarm the piers looking for her, a black and poisonous cloud rolling out over the water, stifling the afternoon sun. She'd be long gone before they arrived. Jenny was not in good shape. She clung to the helm shakily, her head nodding gently as waves of exhaustion rolled through her. Hope told Jenny to fire the engines and guided her on the throttle. The older woman's hands were so slick with sweat she could hardly grip the wheel.

"I'm sorry it has to be this way," Hope said. "This is probably going to be awful for your family."

"Where is Ken?" Jenny whimpered.

"Put on port five." Hope waved at the helm. "Bring the throttle back a bit."

"I have two grown sons," Jenny said. "They have children."

"I don't care."

"Just tell me if Ken is still alive," Jenny pleaded. "Tell me what happened. I have to know."

Hope hardly heard the sick woman at the helm. For many years, Hope had been thinking about people in terms of how they related to her "Circle of Care." A wide ring around her shut people out, or welcomed them in. It encompassed the people who were her responsibility, those she could trust, those it was safe to love. The circle had shrunk a little when she was a child every time her father had beaten her, so that the man had slipped out of it completely over time. When he'd grown old and mild, always moaning about forgiveness and mistakes, Hope hadn't been able to bring herself to pull the man back inside the circle. For a while, in her teenage years, there had been friends and boyfriends inside the circle, but they'd walked out steadily as she'd taken to drinking and partying. When she'd started working in the Cross, she'd looped that small but loving circle around the other girls in her brothel. Together they'd gotten through the long nights and sleepy days, pulled each other up from the depths when it all became too much, watched out for the telltale track marks that meant someone was losing control.

But when Hope had been kicked out of the brothel for hiding profits from her madam, she'd found herself and Claudia the only two people left in the circle. And Hope was so used to people walking out, or being squeezed out, that she had really just been waiting all the time for Claudia's turn to leave. And that turn had come when she'd fulfilled her role in taking down the Spellings. Hope had had no use for her after that. She wasn't part of the glorious plan.

The circle was closed. Strangers like Jenny didn't have a chance. Hope directed the older woman to rev the engines when the bow was pointing to clear, empty horizon. Behind them Hope could see cops arriving on the pier. They'd stopped the taxi driver before he could get out of the marina. It was a close call, but Hope was getting ahead of them. Maybe she'd make it. There were plenty of heavy things on board to tie Jenny to if she got in trouble.

CHAPTER 47

I PICKED A vessel close to the end of the pier and shuffled the old couple who were having tea on the back deck off it. The water police in Sydney Harbor were gearing up, and the coastguard was sending a chopper. The radio I'd taken from a patrol cop at the bank was roaring with dozens of voices coordinating things here and there. A hostage negotiator teaching young criminologists at the University of Sydney was being pulled out of a lecture and driven at top speed towards the coast.

I stopped Tox on the back deck.

"Maybe you should stay," I said.

"What?" he scoffed. "Fuck off."

"Look," I said, "this is our case. We don't want it fucked up by idiot water police guys who insist on ignoring us because you're on board. If you're not around, I've got a chance of having some pull out there. I want control of the situation."

"I'm not leaving this case." Tox pushed me away. "Get on the helm and shut up."

"They're going to fuck with us out there, and lose us our suspect," I said. "Tox, you're a murderer!"

"I'm a killer, not a murderer!" he shouted. "There's a difference, Detective Blue."

I stared at him. He was ignoring me. He worked the helm like an expert, bringing the boat out of its mooring and turning it towards the sea in a seamless glide while its owners railed at us from the pier. I didn't know what to say. He glanced at me.

"I don't care that people don't like me," he said. "I deserve some punishment. But I don't drop cases, and I don't lose suspects."

I opened my mouth to answer, but nothing came out. He gestured to the throttle.

"Get moving." He looked to the horizon. "We've got to catch up and talk her down before she does something stupid and kills the hostage."

The police radio channels separated. I got onto a channel with the water police and Chris Murray. The coastguard hung back and let us take charge, three boats behind a row of five police cruisers and Tox's and my commandeered leisure yacht. We lost sight of land quickly. The freshly painted *New Hope* grew larger as we inched closer.

It was an hour of slow, restless following before Hope finally answered repeated pleas to talk over the radio. She came through loud and clear on the channel reserved for the police.

"I've got Jenny Spelling tied to a compressor," she said. "She's going overboard if you get any closer."

CHAPTER 48

THE COMMAND TEAM, led by Chris Murray, said nothing about Hope's progress out to sea. As long as she was talking, Murray seemed happy to let her trundle on ahead of us. But I wanted Hope to stop. While she was underway, she thought she was shifting closer and closer to being free, and I knew negotiations would last longer while she felt she had the upper hand. Jenny Spelling was sick. She wouldn't last a twelve-hour siege. I shifted in beside Tox at the helm and pointed to the *New Hope*.

"Come up alongside her," I said. "Keep your distance, like she said. Don't get any closer."

I went out of the bridge and down the steps to the back of our vessel. There was a tarp to protect the deck from the rain, hanging over the rear of the galley. I tore that down. I dragged a net out of a box on the deck and then went inside, grabbed sheets and blankets from the bed and lugged them out onto the deck.

Hope's vessel slowly loomed up beside me. All the lights were on. I could see the young woman standing at the helm, looking out. I couldn't make out her expression. Jenny was on the other side of her, just her feet visible near a gap in the wall outside the bridge.

"I don't know what this boat is doing out to my starboard side."

Hope's voice was high with tension on the radio. "But I want them to fuck off."

"What are you doing?" Tox shouted at me.

"Go round the front!"

The engines roared beneath me. I copped a hit of sea spray in the face as the boat lurched over the waves. As we came across Hope's bow, I waited until the right moment and then began hurling the sheets, blankets, tarp, and net into the sea.

"What the fuck?" Hope screamed on the radio.

I hung on as we took a huge wave to the starboard side, crossing over to Hope's port side.

I didn't know if my plan had worked immediately. There was no discernible crunch of the propellers as they became tangled in the debris I'd put right in Hope's path. After a while, I noticed her boat was slowing. There was smoke on the wind.

I looked up in time to see Hope on the port side, standing over Jenny as she lay helpless on the deck. As I watched, Hope looked back towards the boats behind her and raised the radio to her mouth.

"You shouldn't have done that," Hope said. "Now I'll have to punish her."

CHAPTER 49

HOPE UNSCREWED THE silencer and threw it over the side. The gunshot cracked over the ocean, rolling and echoing on the waves. Jenny didn't move. Hope's voice was impossibly high on the radio, the screech of a deranged woman.

"You do not want to fuck with me right now!" Hope said. "This woman is really sick. It won't take more than a couple of shots to finish her off!"

"Fucking psychopath," I seethed. Hope turned and popped off five shots at us. One clanged off the roof of the boat, mere inches from Tox's head. I threw myself to the deck and listened. Tox veered the boat away.

"Good move with the tarps," Tox said as I crawled back into the bridge.

"Detective Blue, that was a damn senseless move," Chris Murray blasted on the radio. He wanted the water police to hear that he didn't agree with the risk I'd just taken, in case it caused Hope to kill her hostage. He also wanted Hope to know she had a good cop to trust, now that it was clear who the bad one was. I switched over to the coastguard channel to talk back to him privately.

"She won't kill her," I said. "Not yet."

"Your actions have caused the hostage injury!" Chris snapped.

"Jenny Spelling didn't move an inch when that gun fired," I said. "I reckon Hope's bluffing. Probably put a hole in the deck. She can't risk the only leverage she's got."

Chris switched back to Hope's channel.

"Hope Stallwood, this is Detective Christopher Murray. The detective who disabled your engines acted completely without authority."

Hope's voice came over the radio: "Detective, your people are going to get an innocent woman killed. Is that what you want? Now you're going to have to provide me with another vessel. If you don't start listening to me I'm going to kill her. Okay? I'm going to murder her right in front of you!"

She was almost screaming. Murray needed to bring her tension levels down before she did anything stupid. I'd raised them to manic level, but it had been worth the risk. The water police and coastguard vessels were slowly maneuvering around the front of the *New Hope,* trying to box her in while she was distracted.

"Hope, we're going to need you to tell us what condition Mrs. Spelling is in," Murray said. "We can't see what's going on. Did you wound her just now?"

There was silence for a long time. Hope was focused on her victim. She wandered down the bridge a little, turned and paced back. Her face was taut. Jenny's legs were moving. I could see her knees jostling through the gap in the bridge wall.

"There's something wrong with her," Hope's voice crackled on the radio, frighteningly calm. "She's having some kind of seizure."

CHAPTER 50

"WHAT EXACTLY'S WRONG with her?" Tox asked.

"Murray said she's got some kind of kidney thing," I said. "I don't think she's had her medication. That's how the family knew something was up. Why they reported them missing."

My whole body ached to be on that boat. Though she wasn't giving us any details, I knew Hope could have wounded Jenny with that gunshot, just to mess with us. The shot could have tipped Jenny over the edge into a seizure.

Hope walked to the end of the upper level of the boat and looked at the vessels ringing her, paced back again and stared at her victim, now still.

"Hope, are you willing to let us send a medic on board?" Murray said.

Hope went to the end of the boat again, lifted her gun and started firing. I ducked, but she wasn't firing at us this time. Murray's boat had been carried forward a little farther than the others as we came to a stop behind the *New Hope,* and she was warning him back. I saw all three officers on board dive for the deck.

"Girl's gonna run out of bullets in a minute," Tox grunted.

He was right. Hope stopped firing and returned to the bridge.

When she reappeared she had a hunting rifle in her hand. She pointed it skyward and fired at the coastguard chopper, which was hovering high above us. She only gave it one shot. This was probably her last gun.

"Move back!" her voice screeched on the radio. Murray put his boat in reverse and came into line with the rest of us.

Every second of growing darkness was agonizing. Jenny wasn't moving. A couple of times, rogue officers on the water police boats tried to creep forward into the circle we'd established around the *New Hope*. But she spotted them soon enough and forced them back.

I could see the air compressor she'd tied Jenny to. A third of the heavy, squat machine was hanging off the edge of the boat, just beyond the gap in the bridge wall. When she felt threatened, Hope would go to the machine and rattle it, push it farther over the edge and then pull it back. I waited for Jenny to move. She didn't.

I couldn't take it any longer. All of the vessels around the *New Hope* had their spotlights trained on the water around the hull. I got an idea, and flicked ours off.

"What's the plan now, genius?" Tox asked.

I switched radio channels onto the coastguard channel, so that Hope couldn't hear me. I radioed the three coastguard boats spread throughout the circle.

"Coastguard, coastguard, this is Detective Harriet Blue, over."

"Coastguard here."

"Can you guys wait a few minutes, then switch your lights off? I'm trying to set up a path in, over."

Hope had noticed I'd switched my spotlights off, and that the ocean in front of my boat was black. I played it casual, leaning on the top of the bridge, talking to Tox. If I was careful, she'd think I was just switching the big light off to conserve my boat's battery power. I could feel her watching me, but she said nothing to Chris about it as they negotiated over the radio.

My plan was working. After a time, one coastguard boat switched off its light. Then another. Hope hardly noticed. She was ranting and pacing.

"You don't fucking understand. You're a man. How could you? You probably grew up in some mansion in bloody Mosman or something. You probably went to private school, didn't you? You were a poor choice of negotiator, my friend. There's no way you could possibly understand me. All right? So don't say that you do."

"We had another negotiator for you." Chris sighed. I could hear his dismay over the radio. "He's been held up."

Half the ocean around the *New Hope* was in darkness. The police boats cut beams of light through the black waves. It was time to go.

"You coming?" I asked Tox. He looked bewildered, until I started taking off my shoes.

"Oh, shit." He sighed, peeling off his jacket.

CHAPTER 51

AS WE SWAM along the side of the *New Hope* to the diving ladder, the sounds of Hope's yelling from the upper decks reached us. We'd dived deep from the back of our vessel, popping up just once in the dark between the boats to breathe. The threat of Hope seeing us and firing into the water made my jaw lock with terror. I pulled my gun out of the back of my pants and put it on the deck in front of me as I got to the top of the ladder. I hoped that if I needed it, it would still work. I didn't know how it would react to the saltwater.

The cold seized everything, made every muscle hard as stone. I stood shivering on the deck as Tox climbed out. We were near a dark, cluttered galley. Our socks squelched on the polished wood. We listened to the voice above us, her footsteps on the floor. Tox was sniffing the air. He went to the pantry and pulled open the door. Leaning against it was a heavy man in a white business shirt. Tox checked his pulse, but he was long gone, his whole body a sickening purple.

"Water safety guy," Tox said. He pushed the limp body back into the pantry and shut the door. "Probably caught on to her."

We crept around the back of the galley and up the stairs, stopping when we were high enough to look across the deck to the bridge wing. Jenny was on her belly now, unconscious. She seemed to be breathing. There were no open wounds on her that I could see, adding hope to my theory that the gunshot earlier had been a bluff. The compressor she was tied to was hanging halfway out over the side of the boat, its small wheels spinning. I could see Hope's leg by the entrance to the bridge. She paced, wandering over to Jenny and then back to the helm, never leaving her alone for more than a few seconds.

"We'll come up the other side," Tox breathed. "Get her from behind."

"We should split up in case she lunges for the compressor. I'll go up this side."

My partner's eyes glittered in the dark. He nodded and checked the magazine in his gun. We were set to go until Hope's voice rose in pitch and volume, stopping us in our tracks.

"Where are the occupants of that boat?" she screamed.

CHAPTER 52

I LOOKED, AND saw her pointing off the port side. It was our boat that had caught her attention. The water police on the vessel beside ours had seen us go into the water and lashed our boat to theirs, but hadn't sent another officer over to cover our absence. Hope had been watching our boat and noticed no one was on board.

"Shit," I whispered.

"The officers who were on that boat moved over to the next one." Chris tried to cover us. He didn't sound confident enough. "They're there, Hope. No one's—"

"Someone's boarded me," Hope snapped. "One of your officers has boarded me, haven't they? You people have no regard for life, do you? I'm going to kill this innocent woman if you don't get your officers off my fucking yacht."

She went to Jenny and actioned the rifle, pointed it at the woman's head. The wind whipped the young woman's hair as she stared out defiantly at the boats around her. I got up on my haunches and got ready to run.

"Hold your fire!" someone yelled on the wind. "Hold your—"

A couple of shots clanged off the edge of the vessel, just above Hope's head. She slid down to her backside and growled with rage.

"Fuckers!" she yelled.

I watched the fury tremble through her, down her chest and through her stomach like electricity in her muscles. It was anger that moved her, taking over and crushing her logic. She kicked out and toppled the compressor over the edge of the boat.

"No, Hope!" I yelled. "No!"

It was too late. I saw the heavy machine go over the side.

CHAPTER 53

THE COMPRESSOR HIT the water with a massive splash. The rope around Jenny's legs whizzed over the side. I sprinted along the deck and reached it just as the rope ran out and yanked the wounded woman off the side of the boat.

I dived in after her, the fifteen feet of free air between the deck and the water feeling like ten minutes of sheer terror before the blackness of the ocean swirled around me.

The water was so cold that for a moment I didn't know if I'd been successful in grabbing at Jenny's hands. I held tight, and as we sailed downward I realized that I had a death grip on one of her wrists. We were sinking fast. There was no sound. The woman in my hands had come to and twisted and bucked as we plunged towards the depths.

We sailed downward. The pressure on my chest and head was too heavy to bear after only seconds. A voice in my head began screaming.

It's over. Let go. Let go. Get to the surface!

But I refused to let go.

CHAPTER 54

HOPE WATCHED THE bubbles rise from where her hostage and the cop had disappeared into the black depths. A couple of officers from boats nearby leaped into the water, diving low to try to help, but Hope knew there'd be no saving them. The deaths were easier now. She hadn't meant to make the compressor go over the edge. The anger had zinged through her, taking possession of her limbs. She was surprised at how little impact the killing made on her psyche. There was a heat, a ringing in her ears, a pounding in her skull, but no regret, no paralyzing sorrow. That was good. If she needed to kill more now to get free, she knew it would be achievable.

"Is she coming up?"

The voice came from behind her. Hope turned and saw a man standing there, the rifle she'd been holding trained on her face. He was soaked through to the skin, blond hair plastered to his forehead, two black eyes and a bruised nose. His face seemed passive, but when Hope didn't answer, he snapped.

"Is she coming up?"

"No."

The man with the gun sneered. "I actually didn't mind that woman."

He turned the gun swiftly and slammed the butt into Hope's jaw. She staggered, and her legs went out from beneath her. She felt teeth wobble in her mouth, swimming in blood. The man must have been a cop. In the spinning world, she saw him go to the edge of the bridge wing and wave at the boats below.

"Suspect down!"

I'll never go down, Hope thought. She reached up while he was distracted by something below, her hand shaking. She slid her index finger into the trigger guard and pulled.

The gun roared, kicked out of his hand. The cop fell.

CHAPTER 55

I'D CLIMBED ALONG Jenny's body, pulling at handfuls of her clothes, and got to her ankle. It seemed years passed as I yanked at the rope. When the weight came free, we hung in the blackness. My eyes were bulging in my skull. She did nothing. The fight had gone out of her. I grabbed, clawed at her neck and head, yanked upward at her arms.

There was water in my lungs. My limbs were starting to shudder. I was drowning. I couldn't tell if we were rising or not. Jenny's hopeless eyes stared up at me. I needed her to kick. Do anything. Keep me down here with her, when every cell in my body was telling me to let go.

Suddenly, she started kicking. We grabbed at each other, pulled upward. The surface came unexpectedly. There were hands under my arms, wrapping around me, dragging me onto my back. I vomited water. Jenny was wide-eyed, being dragged towards the boats by cops.

"Let me go," I said. "I need to get to the boat."

"You're all right now." The officer who had me was trying to pull my head back, relax me, get me to safety. "Take it easy. Breathe."

This was no time to take it easy. I wriggled out of his grip and swam as hard as I could for the *New Hope,* kicking faster as I saw smoke rising from the back deck.

CHAPTER 56

SHE'D GOTTEN HIM in the face, it seemed. The cop rolled away, scrambled until his back was to the helm. He got up, grabbed at the bridge to try to steady himself and knocked the throttle forward. The engine roared and squealed, tugging at the tangled ropes and sheets. Hope went for the gun but he kicked it away and lunged at her, grabbing at her hands, the blood making his fingers slick.

They rolled, twisted, tumbled down the stairs into the galley. His face was a mask of blood, hideous and wet, two cool blue eyes bulging wild as he came for her. Hope grabbed a knife from the kitchen block and threw it, backed it up with a second one. He caught the blade in the air and kept coming. She fell beneath him, the blade inches from her face, and pushed upward with all her might. His blood dripped on her. Her hands slipped, and the knife shunted into the wood right by her ear.

The smoke was sudden, thick with burning chemicals. The wind picked it up from the deck and blew it inside the galley where they fought. The engine had ignited, pushed over its limit by the sheets and ropes tangled around the propellers. The burning fuel seared in their eyes. They both rolled, fighting through the pain, trying to climb to their feet.

Out of the glowing flames on the deck the woman cop emerged, the one who had gone after Jenny. Two other officers were close behind her on the ladder. The woman cop's whole body was shaking with adrenaline and exhaustion. Hope backed towards the stairs as the two officers turned, blocking her exit. She grabbed at the counter, tried to find a weapon. A bottle. A glass. Anything.

"It's over, Hope. The whole thing's going to burn," the woman cop yelled. "Put that down. You've got to come with us."

Hope thought about it. And a weary smile crept to her face at what she imagined, how similar it was to the life she'd lived before. Hands on her. Dark rooms and endless days passing the windows. A team of girls in the prison dorms who'd welcome her, who'd stick by her, cheer her on, try to keep her away from the needle. Sweaty sheets and thin pillows, and those faceless men wandering in the halls, never meeting her eyes, giving her commands.

No. Never again.

Hope went up the stairs and slammed the bridge door behind her.

CHAPTER 57

TOX AND I got off the *New Hope* just in time, falling into the water as one of the fuel tanks exploded and the back half of the yacht listed badly to that side. The water was slick with oil. I was so tired. My arms grabbed weakly at the waves, making no progress, the current trying to push me back against the hull of the burning boat.

Tox pulled my arm around his neck. I held on to his hard, broad shoulders as we swam to the nearest police boat.

As we climbed aboard, we turned to see the fire creeping into the bridge. I could hardly watch. There was no sign of Hope in the blackened windows.

CHAPTER 58

SOMEONE TOOK THE small boat we'd commandeered back to the marina while Tox and I rode home on a police cruiser with Chris Murray. I stood up at the front of the boat with the squat, ruddy-faced man while another officer commanded the helm. Someone had wrapped a blanket around me. But Tox sat unattended at the rear of the boat on a barrel with his own shirt clutched to the gunshot wound in the side of his face. He was watching the boat's wake disappear into the dark of the night.

"You did a sensational job out there," Chris kept saying. Shaking his head ruefully at it all. "You weren't coming up. I was willing to put money on it. You dived in, and you were down there too long, and I thought, *She's got herself tangled up with that woman. She's a goner.*"

"Cut it out." I jabbed him in the side. "You know I don't like it."

We stared at our feet. I knew the answer to my question, but I asked it anyway.

"The husband. Did he make it?"

"No," Chris said.

We shuffled away from the officer driving the boat. Chris's eyes wandered the coastline ahead of us, picking out the clustered lights of Bondi and Coogee and the dark patches where the cliffs met the sea.

"I did look up Tox Barnes," he said suddenly.

"What?"

"Yeah." Chris glanced at me. "After you called me. I felt bad. I knew some guys in records who could pull some strings for me."

"I *knew* you did."

"I thought I'd get the details, just to arm myself, in case you came at me again. I was ready to cut you down about it."

"I don't think I even want to know." I held my hand up. "I think he's all right. And if there was a time when he wasn't all right, well, that seems to have been a long time ago."

"That's the thing." Chris leaned in close. "He *is* all right."

Chris told me the story. It wasn't close to any of the ones I'd heard.

CHAPTER 59

I WENT TO the back of the boat and sat beside Tox as we passed through the heads of Sydney Harbor. Somehow he still smelled of cigarette smoke. One side of his hair was plastered to his head, while the other, where he'd been shot, stuck up in wild spikes. There was blood all through his chest hair.

"How bad is it?" I asked.

"Meh." He shrugged.

He pulled the shirt away. The bullet had carved a vertical line up the side of his face from his jaw to his hairline, burning the flesh on either side, a straight gouge that looked half an inch deep. It was a grisly wound. Something he would wear well.

"Wow, that's disgusting." I reached out. "Can I touch it?"

"Get off." He shoved at me. "Freak."

I looked out at the waves, and the words came easily. Seemed to flow out, unlocked by my exhaustion. I told him I knew about Anna Peake and her son. His victims. I knew that Anna had been heading west on the A32 highway towards Katoomba on a bright Tuesday afternoon when she'd driven under an overpass where Tox Barnes had been standing with a group of other little boys. He was the smallest in the group. Six years old. The oldest had been nine. The boys had been tossing pebbles onto the tops of cars as they drove underneath, cheering and laughing as the rocks clinked and bounced on rooftops and hoods, no idea that what they were doing was incredibly dangerous. They'd gotten over the thrill of raining pebbles on the cars when one of the boys dropped a pebble the size of a penny onto the windshield of Anna Peake's car. The crack of the rock on the glass had been so sudden, so startling, that Anna had swerved and gotten the afternoon sun in her eyes. She had gone across the double lanes and right into the path of an oncoming truck. The boys had rushed to the other side of the overpass and watched her car burn, the mother and her little boy inside.

The five boys had been interrogated by police. The town had called for the oldest boy on the bridge to face criminal prosecution. In the end, none of the boys had been charged. They were so small, and so terrified by the awesome power of their actions, that the police had taken pity on them.

All of the boys had changed their names legally at some point between the deaths of Anna and her son and their adult lives. Terrence Brennan became Tate Barnes. The name change had not destroyed his past completely. Though his involvement in the killings had been suppressed, it had arisen when he'd tried to become a member of the New South Wales state police. The panel of admissions experts who'd approved Tox for service had been obliged to keep his childhood horror a secret. But it had leaked, like all secrets do. It had grown in size, warped, twisted. People had added things. Some had said the boys had stabbed the woman. Beat her. Raped her. Kidnapped her. The boys had grown older. Younger sometimes. New versions of the story had been passed down every year from older cops to the recruits in their charge. Like all rumors, it had its own life. No one knew the truth.

CHAPTER 60

WHEN I'D FINISHED talking I looked at him, expecting something. But he just watched the glowing Harbor Bridge in silence.

"Well?"

"Well what?"

"I need to understand." I held my hands out. "You're innocent. Why do you do this to yourself? Why do you let the rumors go on? Why don't you fix your life?"

"My life's not broken," he said.

"Everybody thinks you're some kind of vicious psychopath."

"This isn't high school." He gave me a pitying glance. "You don't need to worry about what people think anymore."

"You said earlier that you deserve some punishment. Is that how you really feel?"

"A bit." He shrugged. "Mostly, I just let people tell their stories because it keeps them away from me. I've said it from the beginning: I don't work with partners. I'm better on my own."

I watched him, and slowly I began to understand. It was the same as my brother and me, the way we'd acted as kids, running away from the families that tried to take us in, behaving badly and shutting them out until they gave up on us. When we were on our own, we knew what to expect. We knew the rules of the game. Being "included" was risky. Because we didn't accept love and companionship, we couldn't be rejected. Sam and I had known all our lives that we could only rely on each other. Tox Barnes knew it, too.

I was sickened, suddenly, by how familiar I was with it all. Being the outsider. Pushing people away. I had to change his mind. I had to convince him to get his story out there.

"You take pride in what you do. Don't your victims deserve the best from you?" I said. "Your colleagues hate you. They throw up barriers every time you try to make a move on cases. If people knew the truth about you, you'd be a more effective cop."

He actually laughed.

"No, I wouldn't," he said. "I'd end up being a cop like you."

"And what's wrong with that?"

"Oh, man, you have no idea how ineffective you are," he said. "Waiting for autopsy reports. Calling the lab. Talking to colleagues. Hugging the victim's parents. You're a part of the system, mate. I'm outside the system. No one wants to take responsibility for me, so I do what I want. Skip the procedural bullshit. Makes me a better cop than you, I'll tell you that much."

I shook my head at him. It hurt, but I understood. He was pushing me away now, trying to annoy me so I'd leave him alone. I'd done the same thing all my life. Whenever someone uncovered the truth, made me vulnerable, I'd shut them down as hard and as fast as I could.

I walked back to the front of the boat and left him alone.

CHAPTER 61

I'D SLEPT WELL. The first night, it had been sheer physical exhaustion. Every limb had hurt. After I'd been checked over at the hospital, I'd gone home and crashed on my bed face first and slept until the next afternoon.

A couple of nights later I'd followed Matthew Demper and Alex Loris to a bar in Paddington and waited all night while the Kings Cross police officers got themselves nice and tipsy playing pool and betting on the horses. When they returned to their car, I'd given them a few seconds to remember me as the detective they'd made jump out of a police van with her hands cuffed behind her back. When their memory was jogged, I'd broken Demper's nose and given Loris a sound kick to the nuts. I slept even better after that.

I was all ready to take my place on the Georges River task force. It was the perfect moment, and I'd make sure Pops knew that. Nigel had called a press conference with the national media, telling them he had some big announcement with regard to the case. I walked into the station, planning to tell him that he could announce that he was adding me to the task force while he was at it. How could they refuse me now? The newspapers were lauding me as a national hero. For once in my career I was in a position to make demands. And I was going to demand a spot on the hunt for that killer.

I strode across the bullpen on the way to Pops's office, knowing Nigel would be in there being briefed about the press conference. I veered off my path slightly when I saw Tox standing by the coffee machine, half his face swathed in bandages, scratching at the bottom of a jar of coffee with a spoon. I marched up and slapped his arm.

"I'm about to burst in and put myself on the Georges River task force," I said. "Did you hear there's going to be some kind of announcement?"

Tox looked at me. His characteristic blankness had lifted slightly. There was a look in his eyes that was almost concern.

"You haven't met with the Chief yet? Does he know you're here?"

"No," I said. "What's wrong? Is it the announcement? Do you know what it is?"

Tox looked over my shoulder. The Chief was heading towards me, fast. The way he put his hand gently on my shoulder sent my stomach plunging. This was a man who'd broken my tooth in the boxing ring. He didn't touch me that way. No one did.

"I need to see you," Pops said. "Could you give me a few minutes, and then come sit down? We need to talk."

"In your office?"

"No," he said. "In the interrogation room."

CHAPTER 62

IT WAS THE hardest thing he'd ever had to do. And that was a hell of a statement, because what was "hard" in the job had changed incredibly over Chief Morris's career. When he had been a young patrol cop back in the seventies he'd thought the hours were hard, sneaking into the house late at night so he didn't wake the kids. When he'd first made detective, he'd thought finding the bodies of stupid young gang members with their throats cut was hard. It got to be so that the old man had seen such wicked stuff in his time…

But sitting his best detective down and telling her this news, now that was a whole new level.

Detective Harriet Blue sat across from him in the interrogation room, the lights making her look even more tired than she was, her angular head of scruffy hair balanced in one palm. She looked this way in the boxing ring. On the verge. Wired. Ready for the next strike, whether it was his or hers.

The Chief had a tough time trying not to think like her father sometimes. If he'd been her father he'd have kicked her out of the force a long time ago. Got her into something that suited that brilliant mind but wouldn't leave her a bitter, damaged old woman at the end of her career. He'd have dragged her out of the academy by her hair if he'd had to. But he wasn't her father.

The words came out slowly. He danced around the issue for a bit. Then he laid it on her straight, the way she deserved.

"We found the Georges River Killer," he said.

He looked at her eyes.

"It's your brother, Blue. It's Sam."

Harriet twitched, just once, the way she would do when he'd smack her good and hard in the boxing ring. She was trying to work out what had just happened.

Her sharp, cold eyes examined his.

Then she got up and left.

CHAPTER 63

HE FOUND HER in the Georges River Killer task force room, of course. She'd finally busted her way in. When Chief Morris came through the door, he saw exactly what he expected. The short, wiry Detective Blue was going at her nemesis Nigel Spader with all the blind ferocity of a Jack Russell terrier. Above her on the case board the evidence she'd been blind to in the months since the killings had started fluttering a little in the fray. All the officers in the room were silent. Some were half-heartedly trying to pull the woman off her victim.

"How could you be so completely wrong?" Blue howled. "How could you be so completely, completely *useless!* You pathetic piece of—"

"That's enough!" Chief Morris stepped forward, took Blue's arm. He felt her shaking. "Detective Blue, you get a hold of yourself right now or I'll have the boys escort you out onto the street."

Blue whirled around and looked at him. The shock and heartache of a betrayed kid, eyes wide, disbelieving, all the exhaustion of the former case now vanished from her features. Her cheeks were flushed and her teeth gritted. Just as she did when she came around from a near-knockout in the boxing ring, Chief Morris watched as she shook it off and set her mind to what she'd do next to survive. She shoved past him. He felt the gentle brush of her shoulder like the slam of a sledgehammer.

That's it, Blue, he thought. *You're not done yet.*

When she'd gone, the case room was somber. The men standing there looked silently at him, waiting for direction. Yes, none of them had ever been on the friendliest of terms with the little firecracker in their station. Harriet Blue was too determined, too brash, too obsessed with the job to fit in with these guys. But they still didn't like having to do this to her. How could anyone? A sex crimes detective's brother turns out to be the worst homicidal sexual predator in decades, maybe ever. Pops felt the humiliation. It was thick as smoke in the air.

He went to the case board and looked at the photographs there, interior shots of Samuel Jacob Blue's apartment taken during the search. Grainy surveillance images of the beloved brother walking in the street on the night of the first victim's murder, hundreds of meters down from her apartment, a dark ball cap pulled down over his face. The Chief absentmindedly pulled down fingerprint analysis from the first two victims. Turned it over and over in his hands, uncertain.

"We're right, aren't we?" he said aloud, his eyes wandering over the huge collection of evidence. He found that his throat was tight. This was really hitting him. It had been years since he'd felt this troubled.

"We're right," Spader said, taking the sheet from him and pinning it back on the board. "It's him. He's the killer. We checked and double-checked. And after we make an arrest, we'll get a confession. It won't take long. There's nothing you can say in the face of this stuff." He gestured to the board. "It's open and shut."

"It better be," Chief Morris said. If it was all a mistake, and they'd brought in an innocent man, the Chief was sure he'd have lost one of the greatest investigative minds he'd seen in his policing career. Blue wouldn't come back to the force that had turned against her. She wouldn't trust him anymore, his people. It had been enough of a mission to get her settled in the first place. She wasn't good with institutions. They'd mishandled her as far back as she could remember.

But worse than all that, all the embarrassment and mistrust, all the heartache and accusations and damage it would do to Blue and her relationship with the force, if they were wrong about Samuel Jacob Blue, it would mean one thing. That the monster was still out there. And they had no idea who he was.

Harry had taken down the central picture in the case board, a photo of her and her brother, their faces pressed together. It would be puzzling for her, how her brother could be such an evil being when every cell in her own body was inherently good. The Chief knew the answer. It wasn't about good and evil—it was about fire. It took a white-hot flame in a sick, terrible mind to drive Sam Blue to do what he did. So much energy. So much destruction. The Chief had seen that fire in the eyes of plenty of horrible men. He'd seen it most in the ghouls who lurked in the back of prison cells, those vicious dogs who were deemed unfit to ever reenter society. He'd seen it burning, too, in the eyes of heroes he'd worked with on the job, the cops who got up and rushed towards the sounds of screaming when everyone else was taking cover.

That same fire burned in Detective Harriet Blue. The Chief knew her brother's arrest wouldn't put it out. It would make it burn brighter.

ABOUT THE AUTHORS

JAMES PATTERSON has written more bestsellers and created more enduring fictional characters than any other novelist writing today. He lives in Florida with his family.

CANDICE FOX is an award-winning crime writer based in Sydney. She is the author of three crime novels—*Hades, Eden,* and *Fall*—and, with James Patterson, cowrote the thriller *Never, Never.*

HER HUSBAND HAS A TERRIBLE SECRET....

Miranda Cooper's life takes a terrifying turn when an SUV
deliberately runs her family's car off a desolate Arizona road. With
her husband badly wounded, she must run for help alone as his
cryptic parting words echo in her head: "Be careful who you trust."

COME AND GET US

BY JAMES PATTERSON
WITH SHAN SHERAFIN

**Read the heart-pounding thriller,
available now from**

BOOKSHOTS

GOD SAVE THE QUEEN—ONLY PRIVATE CAN SAVE THE ROYAL FAMILY.

Private is the most elite detective agency in the world. But when kidnappers threaten to execute a Royal Family member in front of the Queen, Jack Morgan and his team have just twenty-four hours to stop them. Or heads will roll…literally.

PRIVATE: THE ROYALS

BY JAMES PATTERSON
WITH REES JONES

Read the brand new addition to the Private series, available now only from

BOOK**SHOTS**

"I'M NOT ON TRIAL. SAN FRANCISCO IS."

Drug cartel boss the Kingfisher has a reputation for being violent and merciless. And after he's finally caught, he's set to stand trial for his vicious crimes—until he begins unleashing chaos and terror upon the lawyers, jurors, and police associated with the case. The city is paralyzed, and Detective Lindsay Boxer is caught in the eye of the storm.

Will the Women's Murder Club make it out alive—or will a sudden courtroom snare ensure their last breaths?

Read the shocking new Women's Murder Club story, available now only from

BOOK**SHOTS**

MICHAEL BENNETT FACES HIS TOUGHEST CASE YET....

Detective Michael Bennett is called to the scene after a man plunges to his death outside a trendy Manhattan hotel—but the man's fingerprints are traced to a pilot who was killed in Iraq years ago.

Will Bennett discover the truth?

Or will he become tangled in a web of government secrets?

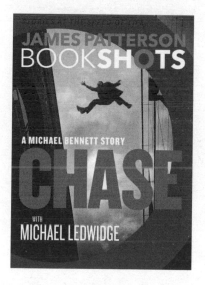

Read the new action-packed Michael Bennett story, *Chase*, available now only from

BOOKSHOTS

SOME GAMES AREN'T FOR CHILDREN....

After a nasty divorce, Christy Moore finds her escape in Marty Hawking, who introduces her to all sorts of experiences, including an explosive new game called "Make-Believe."

But what begins as innocent fun soon turns dark, and as Marty pushes the boundaries farther and farther, the game just may end up deadly.

Read the new jaw-dropping thriller *Let's Play Make-Believe*, available now from

BOOKSHOTS

Looking to Fall in Love in Just One Night?

Introducing BookShots Flames:

Original romances presented by James Patterson that fit into your busy life.

Featuring Love Stories by:

New York Times bestselling author Jen McLaughlin

New York Times bestselling author Samantha Towle

USA Today bestselling author Erin Knightley

Elizabeth Hayley

Jessica Linden

Codi Gary

Laurie Horowitz

…and many others!

Available only from

HER SECOND CHANCE AT LOVE MIGHT BE TOO GOOD TO BE TRUE....

When Chelsea O'Kane escapes to her family's inn in Maine, all she's got are fresh bruises, a gun in her lap, and a desire to start anew. That's when she runs into her old flame, Jeremy Holland. As he helps her fix up the inn, they rediscover what they once loved about each other.

Until it seems too good to last…

Read the stirring story of hope and redemption
The McCullagh Inn in Maine, **available now from**